Unwrapped

Rachel Rowan

Please visit www.rachelrowan.com to sign up to Rachel Rowan's newsletter and for more information on her books.

Unwrapped

Published 2023

1st Edition

Copyright © Rachel Rowan 2023

The right of Rachel Rowan to be identified as the author of this work has been asserted in accordance with sections 77 and 78 of the Copyright Designs and Patents Act 1988.

This book is a work of fiction. The characters and events in this book are fictitious and any resemblance to actual persons, living or dead, is purely coincidental and not intended by the author.

No part of this book may be reproduced in any form or by any electronic or mechanical means, including information storage and retrieval systems, without written permission from the author, except for the use of brief quotations in a book review.

Contents

Author's note	V
Dedication	VI
1. Chapter 1	1
2. Chapter 2	10
3. Chapter 3	17
4. Chapter 4	23
5. Chapter 5	33
6. Chapter 6	42
7. Chapter 7	50
8. Chapter 8	60
9. Chapter 9	65
10. Chapter 10	75
11. Chapter 11	81

12. Chapter 12	89
13. Chapter 13	99
14. Chapter 14	105
15. Chapter 15	115
16. Chapter 16	122
17. Chapter 17	140
18. Chapter 18	146
19. Chapter 19	156
Epilogue	169
Thank you	176
Have you tried...?	177
Books mentioned in Unwrapped	180
Acknowledgements	182

Author's note

This story is a standalone, but in the context of the Entitled Love world it starts after the events of *Unwanted* and before the events of *Engaging the Enemy*.

This book uses British English spellings, e. g. "realised" instead of "realized" and "travelled" instead of "traveled". I promise they are not typos.

For the book nerds.
Takes one to know one ;)

Chapter 1

WILLIAM AUGUSTUS HENRY SHILSTONE the Second—known simply as Biffy—stood on the minstrel's gallery of Castle Deveron, looking down at the banquet hall and Christmas party guests below.

With him were two of his closest friends, Hugo Blackton and Vikram Singh. All three of them took note of the couple that entered the banquet hall and stopped just inside the door, hand-in-hand. The man, Jay Orton, was another of their friends. And the woman with him was his girlfriend, Sophia.

"All of the kings," muttered Vikram, "dropping like flies."

Vikram was on Biffy's right, both of them leaning their forearms on the balustrade of the gallery balcony. Hugo was on Biffy's left, one hip against the rail, his arms crossed. Another couple moved through the glittering party crowd. Biffy's cousin, Edward, and their host, Natalie, owner of Castle Deveron.

"What's the betting," Hugo said with a grimace, "that someone pops the question before next year is out?"

Vikram grunted, eyes back on Jay, who was smiling,

leaning close to talk into his girlfriend's ear. "Please tell me the condition isn't terminal. I need hope things are going to get back to normal."

Biffy raised a doubtful eyebrow, but let their conversation slide past him, preferring to lose himself in the glow of the roaring log fire that gilded the ancient, smooth stones of the floor below. Lights nestled among the holly and the ivy that was, quite literally, decking the hall. Through it all rose the scent of fresh-cut winter greens and the fire's woodsmoke, mingling with the voices, the laughter, and stirring the heat of whisky in his chest.

His expression might have been mimicking the same bemused contempt as his friends, but really he was watching the picture perfect scene like a child hunting through heaped presents under the tree. Searching for the one that was his—or the one he hoped to make his.

Fel—Felicity Pennington—was meant to be here. But he couldn't see her among the guests, the bright, shimmering crowd of sequinned dresses and dark suits. *A small party,* the word had been. Just Edward and Natalie and a few close friends. *A small, informal Christmas party, to warm the house up a bit.* But Natalie was the new Marchioness Banberry, and she was an *actress*, and Deveron hadn't been opened to visitors in decades, so of course everybody who was anybody wanted to come and see it all for themselves. Or maybe they just wanted to see if the rumours were true. Edward Ashley was going steady. Edward Ashley had been caught.

Then the infamous Jay Orton went the same way. And, of course, everybody in the world had to see *that* with their own eyes. Because who would believe it otherwise?

Hugo cast a dark look in Biffy's direction. "You'd dive over and join them if you could, wouldn't you, Biff?"

"Is she even coming?" asked Vikram. Despite Biffy's best efforts, his unrequited crush on Felicity Pennington was far from secret.

"She told Jules she was," he said. "And Jules told Jay."

"Pathetic," scoffed Hugo.

He had been looking at Jay and Sophia as he spoke. And his comment might have been aimed at them. But he turned to look at Biffy, making it clear who he meant.

"There's a dozen girls down there. And you're so hung up on Fel that you're going to miss your chance with any of them. As always."

Biffy kept his face impassive and raised one shoulder in a careless shrug. "What can I say? She's at the top of my Christmas wish-list."

"Your to-do list," said Vik.

"Forget the list," urged Hugo. "Rummage through the stocking fillers."

They didn't get it. That one girl could be different from all the rest. That a girl could make your breath catch, make the rest of the world turn dim. The first time he saw Fel, almost eight years ago, he'd stared, helplessly caught. She was tall and lithe and graceful, a sheet of dark mahogany hair, big doe-brown eyes... That's exactly what she was like: a shy forest creature, a nymph, an elf-maiden... He sometimes dreamt of her walking towards him through the dappled shade of a green-lit forest, nothing but long bare legs and a few strategically placed leaves, those pool-dark eyes on his as a smile played over her lips...

Try explaining *that* to guys like Hugo and Vik. Guys he'd known since he was eighteen, and been instantly in thrall to because they were who he wanted to be. All taller and wilder and bolder and better looking. Guys people turned to look at when they walked into a bar or a club. Hugo's smile and model good looks, Vik's debonair cruelty, Jay's ruinous, lost boy charm... But him? He could walk into a room entirely unremarked. He was average height, average build, medium brown hair, eyes that were neither quite grey nor quite blue. The only thing he had in excess was money, so he'd been happy to grease the wheels of his friends' exploits, stock the booze, host the parties... Anything, so long as he got to tag along. Feel like he was one of them.

Pathetic. Hugo was right.

He spotted a face in the crowd. Jules Orton. Jay's sister, but, more to the point, Felicity's best friend. Like usual, she was scowling and dressed all in black. About as inviting as a lump of coal in the bottom of one's stocking. But if anyone knew where Fel might be, it would be Jules.

Affecting a grin, he slapped his hands on the balustrade rail. "Enough moping, everyone. Why are we up here, when the party is down there?"

Jules Orton was in a bad mood. She was at a party, which was not her preferred habitat. Plus, everyone was acting weird. Her brother most of all.

He was across the hall, standing with a beautiful blonde—which wasn't the strange thing. Beautiful women were very much Jay's preferred habitat. The weird thing was that the woman, Sophia, was his *girlfriend*. And Jay was...*glowing*. A gleam in his eyes that she'd never seen before. Jules didn't trust it.

Jay wasn't romantic. None of the Ortons were. They were constitutionally incapable of it. Any faith in romance and love and happy-ever-afters had been well and truly scorched by their parents' example.

Marriage? Love? They were toxic. And all men were terrible. She was sure of that.

"Jules! Just the person I've been hoping to see."

She turned to find one of her brother's friends. And, no surprise, he was lying. Men always did. The only person he wanted to see was Jules' best friend, Felicity Pennington.

"William," she said without enthusiasm.

"You know you can call me Biffy? We've known each other for years."

"I don't want to call you Biffy. It's a stupid name that makes you sound like a clown."

A frown flickered across his face. Something that might have been hurt. But it was immediately replaced by a smile as he attempted to laugh it off. He was always smiling, smiling, smiling. Good old Biffy. Desperate to be everyone's friend.

In many ways, he was the least worst of her brother's cronies. Except, somehow, that made him the most irritating. He was the one who always got on her nerves. The one she wanted to take hold of and shake. The others were intrinsically awful. William pretended to be by choice.

It was very, very annoying. Because he was better than that.

She tried to soften her tone, relenting a little. She even attempted a smile, though she wasn't much in the mood for it, and it probably came out more like a grimace. "I know that for some unfathomable reason, you strive to be seen as a clown, but I feel honour-bound to point out it isn't doing you any favours. Consider that my Christmas gift to you." She turned back to watch the crowd, feeling the tiniest bit of guilt about the second frown that flashed over his good-natured face. It looked wrong against his faint freckles, his boy-next-door good looks.

"Not sure you've quite got a handle on the whole Christmas thing, Jules."

He said it softly, a little dry. A flush spread up her neck.

"She's not here," she said quickly. "Fel. She was meant to be. She told me she would be. But she's not. She's gone straight home to Kent."

That was the other reason she was in an even worse mood than usual. Only two things had convinced her to attend this party. One was Jay asking her to, so that Sophia might have some familiar faces around her. And the other was Fel promising to come. She was studying veterinary science in Edinburgh and had said she would drop in to see Jules and her cousin, Sophia, given Castle Deveron was near Aberdeen, not too far away.

But no.

"Clarence is lame, apparently," she told William.

"Clarence?"

"Her pony. He lives back home in Kent. He's about a million years old. She's had him forever and she loves him more than life itself. Sorry, William. You can't compete with that."

She glanced at him to find his cheeks tinged pink. He fidgeted a little with the glass tumbler in his hand. "Right," he mumbled, then took a large swallow of his drink, seeming at a loss for what to say.

She considered him for a moment. The light brown hair cut short and neat at his neck, a little longer and tousled on top. The straight set of his shoulders in his closely tailored tuxedo jacket. He was a few inches taller than her, so she was looking up slightly at the angle of his jaw, his mouth. He had temporarily forgotten to smile, his blue-grey eyes staring abstractedly out across the crowded hall, settling on Jay and Sophia. Which made him sigh.

He was far less objectionable like this, away from his friends, a little unmoored without that boisterous, bantering crowd around him. She wondered if Jay's defection to blissful coupledom was as weird for him as for her.

"What do you think?" She nodded in their direction. "Do you see it lasting?"

William sipped his drink, taking the question more seriously than she'd expected. "Maybe. Why not?"

"Because nothing ever does."

It came out more bitterly than she'd meant. And unfortunately, it drew William's full attention. She wanted to escape the way he stared, the edge of surprised pity in his gaze.

She found herself wishing, too, that she wasn't dressed

like the moody emo teenager she no doubt sounded like. She was in the blackest and skinniest of her skinny black jeans, knee-high biker boots, and a black silk Chinese-style top with a black embroidered dragon winding around her chest, mirroring the one she sometimes dreamt of getting tattooed onto her skin but knew she never would.

An awkward girl. Trying to look tough.

Failing.

With a quick, dismissive wave of her hand in her brother's direction, she said, "He has no idea what he's doing. He'll get bored in two months. She'll get her heart broken. He'll move on to the next victim. The world will keep turning. So on and so on, *ad infinitum*. There are no happy endings. It's a myth."

"You don't..." He looked embarrassed to be asking. "You don't...believe in love?"

"Not the fairytale ever-after kind in stories."

Not even here, in this castle at Christmas, with wintergreen wreaths draping the ancient walls and firelight flickering over champagne glasses. It was *made* for fairytales. For walks in the snow, and kisses under mistletoe, and limbs twining on a rug before the fire's flames...

She pulled her eyes away from the unusually serious line of William's mouth and gestured once more to the milling, laughing party guests, as though their very existence explained her reasoning.

"I had this exact conversation with Fel. Sorry to say it, but she's as much of a cynic as me. You know she's training to be a vet? She did some modules on animal behaviour. Love is just chemicals and imprinting and pheromones and stuff. Even those stories about animals mating for life are exaggerated. They're mostly all just cheating on each other, spreading their genes around, always looking for the better mate. It's inherently selfish, pairing up. It's only done to improve the chances of any offspring surviving—to preserve that parent's own genes in the next generation. Love is just the chemical brain goo that makes putting up with someone else seem tolerable."

Or that's more or less what Fel had said. Jules wasn't sciencey. She'd studied English Lit.

William stared at her with a different kind of concern. As though she was mad rather than merely sad. But what did she care? Men like him and his friends were the worst examples of the animal kingdom at its most brutish and stupid. Their entire existence was dedicated to spreading oats.

"I think..." he said gently. "There might be other ways of looking at it."

Suppressing a scowl, she just shrugged, starting to make her escape, only for William to be rescued from her. Hugo and Vik arrived, a cluster of girls in tow, and swept William off and out of the hall to some debauched corner of the castle.

Fel had it right. Forget men. Save your heart for a horse.

But when her eyes found her brother in the crowd again, he was looking at Sophia like she was the only thing in the world that mattered. The gleam in his eyes looked like joy. And Jules felt a twinge.

She was scared to admit it felt like longing.

Chapter 2

IT SNOWED IN THE night. Just a light dusting. Enough to remind the world that this was Scotland, the distant north, and the Arctic Circle was closer than anyone thought.

Apparently the northern lights sometimes made an appearance here. Edward had told him so, brimful with pride, as though every exotic aspect of this latitude was his girlfriend's doing.

Girlfriend? That sounded too young, too frivolous, for the partner of a man of thirty-two. But what else could Biffy call her?

That name makes you sound like a clown.

He stood at the window a while longer, no longer seeing the dusting of white over the infinite grounds, but Jules, and her casual, unintentional scorn as she stated what was surely a fact to everyone but him.

He had seen the same thing all night long, sleepless and unhappy. Jules telling him he was a clown. That love was a myth.

He hadn't even been able to drink himself free of the memory of it. Hugo and Vik had tried—Hugo in particular going hard at it all night, the way he often did of late, making Biffy suspect he was attempting to escape his own demons.

Maybe on a different night, when he wasn't already filled with helpless disappointment over Felicity's absence, he would have been able to shrug off Jules' barbs. But he had been in a strange mood even before his conversation with her.

Jay's sudden change in relationship status had unsettled all of them. It was like the lights being switched on at the end of a raucous night, suddenly forced to confront the mess, the bottles leaking beer on the floor, the drunks passed out in the corner. Realising that while it might have been fun, it wasn't anything to be proud of. Not in the cold light of day.

Though maybe the feeling had been brewing for month. Definitely Hugo had been unsettled for a while. Ever since the summer and that fiasco with his neighbours, the B-T girls. Biffy only knew the vaguest details, but it had been enough to make him look at his friend askance and wonder, on some barely voiced unconscious level, just what the hell they were all doing? All of them now twenty-six, twenty-seven, no longer the teenagers they'd been when they met at Oxford.

But still acting like it.

He shook his head and headed to the shower, suddenly desperate to leave this place. To go home. It was only eight in the morning. His friends wouldn't be up for hours, but he had a long drive ahead of him. He'd promised his parents to be at their house in Berkshire this evening. Tomorrow was Christmas Eve.

Fifteen minutes later, he was packed, his suit in its cover over one arm, his leather overnight bag in his other hand. He left the room without a backwards glance and headed down in search of breakfast.

Breakfast, his host Natalie had told him the day before, would be in the breakfast room, funnily enough. And he was to ask the kitchen for whatever he wanted.

He remembered the way easily enough. One got used to finding one's way around monstrous houses. But he stopped dead in the doorway.

Jules was there. Only Jules. No one else.

She caught his arrival out of the corner of her eye and lifted her gaze from the book she was reading, a piece of toast in her other hand. She gave a small start at the sight of him. He knew how she felt. But it was too late to run.

He fixed a smile to his face and walked into the room. "Morning, Jules."

"Hi."

He stopped at her table, opposite her. "May I join you?" His parents had raised him to be polite. He often wished they hadn't.

Her smile was tight. "Sure."

She glanced back at her plate as he put his bag down and hung his suit over the next chair. Then she fiddled with her book. Picked it up. Turned a page. Put it down again.

Her hair was tied back in a loose ponytail. The same

shade of brown as Jay's. Her eyes were grey like his, too. They all had a certain look, the Orton siblings. But her eyes were paler, strikingly so. And her face was softer, sweeter, than her brother's. Ironic, really, given her personality was anything but.

Like the rest of the Ortons, she was also absurdly attractive. But she was Jay's sister, so he'd got used to ignoring the fact. This morning, though, he couldn't help but notice she looked tired. As though she, too, hadn't slept well. Or maybe he was just struck by how different she looked to last night. No make-up now. No heavy flicked-out eyeliner, no scarlet lip. Just soft hues of peach and pink. And those silver-grey eyes.

Everything about her was much softer than last night. As though she was no longer dressed ready for battle, her defences down. She was wearing the same biker boots, but her tight jeans were faded to grey. Even her jumper was enormous and fluffy, a shade somewhere between pink and brown. Taupe? Fawn? To his tired eyes, it looked extremely comfortable. He could imagine resting his head on it. Just the jumper folded up to form a pillow, of course. *Not* his head resting on the slender curve of her shoulder—

Her eyes flicked up to where he was still standing motionless by his chair. God. He had practically zoned out. He badly needed coffee.

Jules gestured to a sideboard. "There's cereal, tea, coffee, over there, but the lady in the kitchen said to let her know what cooked stuff you want. There's a phone."

"Cereal's fine," he said, pulling on a smile as he turned to walk to the sideboard. "No point putting anyone to trouble. She'll be rushed off her feet soon." But the curious look Jules gave him made him pause. "What?"

"I don't know. It's just...considerate."

"Not getting a cooked breakfast?"

"Yeah."

"I feel offended that surprises you so much," he said, making sure he was smiling as he said it.

"It's just... You know... Guys like you..." She gave a pointed shrug, as though that explained everything.

"Guys like me?"

"And Hugo and Vikram... You're all so..." She waved her half-eaten toast in the air, as though that, again, made her point clear.

"So...?" he prompted.

She held his gaze for a moment, then something crossed over her face. Doubt, or hesitation. Whatever it was, it made her relent. "Nothing. Never mind."

He crossed over to the sideboard, suspecting she'd decided that whatever it was she'd been about to say was too mean, even for her. Or at least this early in the morning. Maybe after a drink, in the heat of a crowded party, she wouldn't have held her tongue.

It's a stupid name and it makes you sound like a clown.

He knew what she thought anyway. That he was spoilt. Selfish. Thoughtless. Arrogant. Unprincipled. Uncaring.

I'm not like them, he protested in his mind. *I'm not like my friends.*

But hadn't he spent nearly a decade trying to prove the opposite?

He poured himself a strong coffee. Existential confusion

was turning out to be rather taxing.

When he returned to his seat, Jules was looking at her phone, her book abandoned on the table. He studied the cover as he sat down, trying to puzzle it out. It was black—no surprise there—and the main image seemed to be a pair of torn and bloody black-feathered wings, crow wings, or a dark angel. There was also a rusted sword and some twining roses, their petals bruised and falling.

Was it a horror story? A fantasy? It didn't seem like the sort of fantasy books he'd grown up reading, all swords and sorcery and wise, bearded wizards. And noble farm boys. Somewhere, on a dusty memory stick in his boyhood bedroom, were half a dozen attempts at writing a book of his own. They all featured average-looking teenaged farm boys with medium brown hair and blue-grey eyes who suddenly got called to greatness. And met extremely beautiful elf girls and forest nymphs along the way. Nubile and shy and giggling, and mostly naked, and only too happy to deflower the heroic farm boy. He'd never managed to finish writing a single story. Probably because he kept stopping to have a wank.

Also, they were terrible stories.

Jules made an angry noise, tossing her phone down on the table. She caught him staring at her book and grabbed it, shoving it into the bag by her feet.

"Problem?" he asked, pretending the book thing hadn't happened.

"Stupid taxi won't get here in time to get me to the station. I'm going to miss my train. Not that it matters. They're all messed up anyway because of the four millimetres of snow we had last night."

"You're getting the train? To York?"

She hesitated. "To Kent. I'm staying at the Penningtons' for Christmas. I often do."

She didn't need to explain why. He knew from Jay what life at Rakely House was like.

The Penningtons'. Fraversham Hall in Kent. Where Felicity was, right now.

"How about I drive you?" he said.

Chapter 3

THERE WAS A FIRE in the grate in the breakfast room. Jules heard it crackling clearly in the silence that followed William's offer.

It should have been a cosy sound, even though she suspected the profusion of crackling log fires in this castle was as much for practical reasons as festive ambiance.

There was a distinct chill in the air. Everyone said this place had been a wreck, and there were signs of it everywhere, closed off corridors and builder's dust in the corners. Piles of rubble in the yard, the smell of new paint in the room she'd slept in.

She picked up her toast crust as William waited for her answer.

"It's hundreds of miles."

"About eight hundred," he agreed.

"It'll take hours."

"Maybe ten, depending on the traffic. But so would the train. Longer, if there are delays."

"I can't ask you to drive that far."

"I'm driving to Berkshire anyway. It's only a bit further."

Berkshire. Herlingcote Park. His parents' house. She'd been there several times, most recently this summer for another of his ridiculously extravagant birthday parties. He was a generous host, she could acknowledge that much.

"You don't want to be stuck on a broken-down train," he persisted. "Or on a freezing platform, waiting for a train that never turns up. Let me drive you. You'll be comfortable and warm, at least."

She had to admit it sounded nice. That his offer was nice. Though she knew the true reason behind it.

"You'd really drive eight hundred miles just for the chance of seeing her?"

His silence was answer enough, and she couldn't help but wonder how that would feel, to have a man like you that much.

Better than *nice*, probably.

William looked across the room, sipping his coffee, apparently absorbed by the shifting embers of the fire. He was embarrassed, she could tell, his cheeks faintly pink, his expression studiously neutral.

He'd come down from his room with his hair still wet from the shower, wearing a dark green jumper over a white t-shirt, faded jeans. Entirely normal. Attractively so. It was that irritating boy-next-door thing again, his gentle, non-threatening handsomeness tricking her brain into thinking he was a welcome and familiar sight, someone she knew well, when she didn't, not really. And most of what she did know was bad.

She still felt sorry for him though. Felicity Pennington wasn't a good choice to fall in love with. She had no interest in men. In women. In romance. In relationships. It wasn't like she objected to them in the same way Jules did. She wasn't jaundiced or cynical or afraid of being hurt. She simply didn't seem to find any of it remotely interesting.

For a while, Fel had spoken often of a guy back home, the son of a local farmer. She'd been meeting up with him, going to his house. Jules had been intrigued. But it had all become clear when it turned out he was involved in the local animal rights group, and Fel had been meeting him only to discuss their protest plans.

Animals were Fel's only real passion.

"Consider it my Christmas gift to you," William said, putting his empty cup down and leaning back in his chair as he levelled a smiling look at her. They were her own words from last night, but said without her venom. "A chauffeur-driven ride to your destination. Heated seats. As many snack stops as you like. You can even choose the music. Within reason."

"But I love Gregorian monastic chants," she deadpanned.

He laughed. "I could probably live with that. No Coldplay though."

"Not a fan?"

"I lived with someone at university who played their album Parachutes every day. On repeat. For a year. Let's just say, I have some lasting trauma."

She smiled at that. Should she let him know Fel loved the band? But the disappointment on his face last night was still too raw in her mind. Causing more would feel like kicking a puppy.

"OK," she said.

"OK? It's a yes?"

"Yes, William. It's a yes from me."

He smiled, genuinely pleased. Of course he was. Fel Pennington was the pot of gold at the end of this eight-hundred-mile rainbow. Even Jules' scowly troll-like presence couldn't tarnish it for him.

"When do you want to leave?" she asked.

"Soon. One more coffee first. Can I get you one?"

"Please. Thanks."

She watched him cross the room. His perfectly average figure. Da Vinci had probably worked out the golden ratios for male anatomy. The angle at which jaw should meet throat and neck meet shoulder. The relative width of shoulder and hip, and the tapering line of torso between them. William would be squarely in the middle of it all. Slim but not skinny, firm but not bulgingly gym-ripped. Quietly and unremarkably perfect—

Normal. She meant *normal*.

"Are you even safe to drive?" she asked as he walked back with a cup in each hand. "How's your blood alcohol level?"

"It's fine," he said, putting her coffee down and giving her a look of mild reproof. "I barely even drank last night."

"Really? I spotted Hugo when I went up to bed, and he was attempting to climb inside a suit of armour. While singing what seemed to be a particularly filthy sea-shanty."

"Eskimo Nell? Or maybe one of the rugby ones. Man's brain is an encyclopaedia of filth. He's never met an innuendo he didn't—"

"—try to bend his end to?"

William spluttered a laugh. "I see you've got the measure of the man."

"Unfortunately so."

But she returned his grin, then busied herself with her coffee, suddenly aware of the brief silence that fell. The sound of the smouldering fire in the otherwise empty room.

"I wonder what time the others will start getting up?" said William with a glance around the room, as though he too was newly aware of their lack of company. The sky through the tall windows was just beginning to lighten, but it looked cold and grey, heavy with cloud. "Probably not before we leave," he answered himself.

"I did see the Count." She shot him a grin. "When I came down to breakfast. He was looming down the corridor towards me, haunting the place like Heathcliff's ghost. I think he had been doing something horrific. Like going to the gym."

William chuckled. "Wasn't it Cathy's ghost?"

"Don't tell me you've read Wuthering Heights?"

"Had to. Was on my course at university."

"And you did...?"

"Eng Lit."

She stared at him, offended. "No. You lot all do...PPE or Economics or something."

He smiled at her over the rim of his coffee cup, but his smile was firm and slightly combative. "Clearly not."

"You chose it because you thought it was going to be easy, right? A doss subject. You don't...like books."

"Sure." He shrugged, setting his cup down and twisting the handle side to side as he gave her a slanting grin. "Let's say that."

There was a pause. She watched him suspiciously for a moment. He waited for her to pick up her own drink before casually offering, "Anyway, Charlotte Brontë's Jane Eyre is a better book, in my opinion. But my favourite Brontë is—"

She swallowed her mouthful of coffee hastily. "Don't you dare say Tenant—"

"Tenant of Wildfell Hall." He grinned. *Winked.* "By Anne Brontë."

"You're ruining literature for me," she grumbled.

He just laughed. He had an annoyingly nice, extremely contagious laugh. Which she refused to catch.

She downed her coffee in one, then stood up and grabbed her bag. "Let's get this ordeal over with."

Chapter 4

Biffy opened the wooden door to the courtyard of Castle Deveron where his car was parked, then quickly closed it again, shutting out the freezing wind and swirling snowflakes.

He exchanged a rueful look with Jules, who was standing next to him, already shivering in her coat. "Good job you're not getting the train," he said. "Suspect they won't be running at all in this."

"Will the roads be alright?"

He opened the heavy wooden door a crack and squinted through the gap before shutting it again. "Should be. There's only an inch or two settled so far. And the main roads will be gritted. Ben can handle these little country lanes."

"Ben? You called your car Ben?"

"It's a Bentley Bentayga," he said defensively. Then conceded, "Yes. Unoriginal."

"But shouldn't it have a girl's name? Like boats do?"

"Benita?"

She snorted. "No."

"Benella?"

"That's worse."

"Bendelina!"

"Get *bent?*"

"You'll change your tune when you're warming your bottom on Ben's leather insides."

"You realise how disturbing that sounds?"

He chuckled. "Absolutely."

She gave him a flat look, though her silver eyes were dancing in amusement and the corner of her mouth was twitching. This trip might be more fun than he'd hoped. They were standing close together in a damp and dim hallway, nothing but a slab of weathered oak door between them and the blizzard. It did little to keep out the cold. But neither of them made a move to open the door and step into the maelstrom.

He nodded at the bag on her shoulder. A single rucksack. "Is that really all your luggage?"

"What can I say? I'm an uncomplicated girl."

He snorted at that. "Physically maybe, but mentally..." He trailed off with a low whistle.

She glared at him, her full bottom lip a pout. He very much doubted she realised how cute she looked when she did that. She would never have done it if she did.

"We're going to have to face it, aren't we?" she said.

"What?"

She nodded to the door. "The longer we wait, the thicker the snow will get."

"Right. Yes. On three?"

She nodded. He counted them down, then swung the door open. Of course, she had no idea where his car was parked. The rows of vehicles all looked the same, smothered in shapeless white. It took him a moment to orientate himself. He blinked snow from his lashes, then grabbed Jules by the wrist and pulled her after him, both of them slipping a little as they hurried, slightly bent, trying to hide their faces from the bitter wind.

He beeped the car open and got her door. She gave him a breathless thanks as she ducked under his arm and clambered inside. He hurried around the front and got in the driver's seat, pulling the door shut thankfully and turning to dump his bag and suit over the back seat. He immediately set to work starting the engine, turning all the heaters on.

He rubbed his chilled hands together as the wipers began scraping the snow from the windscreen. Jules was huddled beside him, bag at her feet, arms folded, hands tucked into her sides.

"It'll warm up soon."

She just nodded, her focus on the dashboard, running her gaze over the car's interior. The leather seats and accents were a deep reddish tan. The rest was a mix of black and grey. He got out his phone and sent a quick message to Jay:

Driving Jules to Kent. Her trains are messed up.

He hadn't expected a reply. Jay wasn't much of an early riser, but the response came straightaway.

Jay: You're a saint. Thank you.
Jay: Soph says it's snowing? Drive safe.
I'll do the opposite of everything you do, he texted back.
Jay: Perfect.

He breathed a faint laugh, then dropped his phone into the tray between the seats. Jules had started to unbutton her coat. It was already getting warm inside the car. He watched her from the corner of his eye as he switched on the sat nav ready for the Penningtons' postcode, feeling a sudden surge of protectiveness. This was Jay's sister. Jay was trusting him to get her there safely. And he was sure he would. He was a sensible, experienced driver, and Ben was built like a tank. But still, it was a new sensation, this older brother protectiveness. He had lots of cousins, but no siblings—wasn't used to feeling like the grown-up one in any given situation. He might host the parties and grease the wheels of his friends' socialising, but they were very much in control of what they did, and when, and why.

Not that Jules was a *little* little sister. She was…twenty-three? Only a few years younger than him. The same age as Fel. They'd been at school together. That's how the two had met. In fact, that's how he had met Fel in the first place. Through Jules. Fel had been visiting Jules at Rakely at the same time as he had been visiting Jay. He'd walked into the living room, and there she'd been, standing at the window, looking out, like a wild bird in a cage wishing for the sky…

He'd immediately wanted to give it to her. He would have given her anything. His heart had leapt to his throat, every thought in his head had stopped. There was only her. Tall and slender, that sheet of mahogany hair falling almost to her waist, swinging as she turned, startled, and found him standing there.

Staring. Staring like a bloody idiot. And too tongue-tied

to say anything. Just like he had been the half-dozen times they'd met over the years since.

Yes. Pathetic was the word.

"Is this where I type the postcode?" Jules interrupted his brooding. She was pointing at the screen on the car's dash.

"Yes. Thanks."

A press of a button later and X marked the spot. The treasure. Felicity's house. The place where she'd grown up. The place she currently was, right now.

Nine hours, forty-six minutes.

He suspected that was optimistic, the weather being what it was.

"You'd really drive eight hundred miles just for the chance of seeing her?"

He hadn't known how to answer Jules. It sounded absurd, didn't it? He would have liked to believe it was romantic. But he suspected things could only be romantic if there were two people involved. That romance only existed *between* people. It wasn't an action you did, but something two people created. Unrequited romance was just...sad.

Fucking hell. His moping was starting to make Heathcliff seem as bubbly as a children's TV presenter.

He set the Bentayga in motion, comforted by the familiar purr of the engine.

Progress was slow. Oh, God. So slow.

Deveron was located about twenty miles west of Aberdeen, and they had to pick their way back east almost all the way to the city to join the A90 southbound. William's beast of a car seemed to be the first vehicle that had ventured the route, the narrow ways through the sparse countryside around Deveron white with pristine snow that hid the verges and blurred the hedges. The snow was falling so thickly, blown so crazily by the wind, that it was hard to see the way ahead.

Jules almost suggested they turn back, wait for it to die down. But William drove slowly and carefully, his quiet competence putting her at ease. There were no other vehicles around to cause a crash, and the Bentayga was so powerful and massive, it seemed like it would be able to cope with any small ditches or obstacles their uncertain path brought them.

After a while, the wind died down. Snow still fell, but much more lightly, tiny flecks of white that melted as soon as they hit the windscreen. The roads grew wider as they neared Aberdeen, the tarmac slushy and wet with grit and melted snow, but perfectly drivable. William still drove cautiously but at a more normal speed. He let out a breath and his shoulders visibly relaxed.

Jules noted it with a mix of gratitude and guilt. But he would have been driving this way anyway on his way to Berkshire. And besides, it was Fel, not her, who he was going all the way to Kent for.

"I have a second Christmas gift to offer you," she said, now the roads required less of William's attention.

"Oh?"

"It's mainly due to gratitude for Ben and his heated seats."

William nodded solemnly. "Told you."

"My gift is: to tell you where you've been going wrong with Fel. With all women, really."

William choked out a shocked laugh. "That's no gift. That would be like...literal torture. You do realise that? Besides, you said enough last night. I have the name of a clown."

"That was just the first of many hints."

"Criticisms."

"Sage advice."

He said nothing, just shot her a disgruntled look, but his shoulders were tensed higher than they had been when he was driving through the blizzard.

"I really do think you should stop calling yourself Biffy though."

"I didn't start it!" he protested. Then sighed. "Fine. OK."

"William?" she asked cautiously.

"Or Will."

"William," she said again, more firmly. "William. Will. Willlliammmm." She let the sound of his name roll around her mouth, pronouncing it with exaggerated care, caressing the vowels.

"OK," he said, embarrassed. "You can stop that now."

She turned in her seat and mouthed it to him breathily, all lips and tongue. "*William.*"

"Please stop it."

"It sounds good though, doesn't it? You like the way it sounds. Admit it."

His cheeks were that delicious shade of pink. The blush

on a fresh old-English apple. "Yes. OK. You make it sound good. But please stop before it gets weird."

"Already sort of weird."

"*You're* weird."

She chuckled. "Not denying it. Just think, ten hours of this, Willy boy."

"Oh God. I might drive us off the Forth Bridge."

"Pretty sure that's a railway bridge."

"Then I plead for mercy instead."

She laughed, shrugging out of her coat. Will had turned the heaters off a while ago, but it was far too warm in this car. She twisted in her seat and put her coat in the back, then sat and regarded him for a moment.

"My next piece of advice—"

"Please don't. I'm serious."

"My next piece of advice," she repeated more loudly, because she was, despite the fun of winding him up, seriously trying to help. "Is to stop trying so hard."

He flashed her a look of consternation. "With Fel? I'm not sure how I could act any more casual, given I've never actually plucked up the courage to talk to her."

"I mean with everybody. Stop trying to please everyone. Stop trying to be friends with everyone. Stop trying to be Mr Popular. Mr Party. It makes you seem needy."

He let out a measured breath. "Are you sure that bridge is railway only?"

"See? You're trying to make a joke, pretend we're having fun, when really you're pissed off."

He didn't speak for a moment. He shifted his grip on the steering wheel, flexing stiff fingers. "What do you want me to say, Jules? You're Jay's little sister. I'm not going to argue with you."

"Why not?"

"Because I don't want to."

"But at this exact moment in time, you're angry with me, and you think I'm a bitch. Go on, *William*, admit it."

"That's not something I'd ever say to any woman."

"See, this is what I mean."

He looked wary. "What is?"

"You're nice. And I mean it in a good way. You seem to be genuinely nice. But you keep pretending not to be."

"Pretending? When?"

"Any time you're with your friends. You act like they do."

"None of my friends would call a woman that."

She flicked a hand, annoyed he was resisting the point she was trying to make. "Well. I don't know. Maybe not that exactly. But I just think... You're better than they are. But I've known you for nearly eight years and I've never wanted to get to know you well enough to confirm it."

"That seems more like your fault than mine."

"No, it's because you've been trying so hard to hide it under a layer of *bantz* and idiocy and...and...toxic masculinity."

He pulled a face at that last expression. Fair enough. It was one of those buzzwords that got tossed around until it lost all meaning. But it was the best she had to summarise what she felt was the issue.

"I'm actually giving you a compliment," she insisted when he didn't reply, his hands tight on the steering wheel, his jaw set. Worst were his eyes, which seemed a little...hunted.

Oops.

What had possessed her to go so far? Why did she even care this much? She could have spoken to him about the weather, had a nap, annoyed him by playing Coldplay, and arrived at Kent with her reputation as a somewhat sane person still intact. *Bye, William. Thanks for the lift. Merry Christmas.* And life would have continued the same as it always had.

Instead, she was apparently psychoanalysing Biffy Shilstone, of all people. Why? So he might have slightly more of a chance with Fel? But he *didn't*. He never would. She wasn't even remotely right for him. It was just so hard to sit back and watch him waste his time. Watch him get hurt.

Instead, she was hurting him herself. Wonderful.

Merry Christmas, William.

She opened her mouth to apologise, but he surprised her by speaking, his voice quiet. "I can't be angry at you, Jules. Not when you're right."

Chapter 5

Biffy—*William*—had been in many embarrassing situations in his life, but this was by far the most excruciating. Having your friend's kid sister eviscerate your personality, lay bare all your darkest fears, and basically inform you that you're hopeless with women, with people in general, was…erm…absolutely fucking mortifying.

"You're right," he said flatly. "I'm needy and pathetic. Congratulations."

"I don't think you're pathetic—"

"I try to buy people's affection because I know otherwise they'd never give me the time of day."

"I just meant—"

"I'm basically a laughingstock. People only put up with me because they want to borrow my yacht—"

"No—"

"Or my jet—"

"Will—"

"Or my helicopter. Though technically it's my uncle's—"

"William! Listen!"

"What? You have some more personality flaws to point out?"

The look he gave her was petty, he knew that. So was the tone of his voice. He nearly apologised, especially when he saw the contrition in her eyes. But wouldn't that be just like him—trying to make everything right, smooth things over. *Smile, smile. Let's be friends.*

"I was trying to say that you seem like a nice guy, when you let yourself be yourself. Away from your friends."

"Nice." He snorted. "Sure. Because that's what girls like. A nice guy. The truth is, nice is basically the *opposite* of hot."

She scoffed. "That sounds like something Hugo might say. No. Vikram."

He scoffed in return. Very mature.

"Women do like nice guys," Jules insisted. "Of course they do. We'd be idiots not to. Like...back there...when you were driving through the snow—"

"Inching along like grandma?"

"Sexist *and* ageist. Marvellous. I was about to say, when you were driving carefully and competently and keeping the both of us safe... That was...kinda hot."

He shot her a look. "Hot? Driving incredibly slowly and looking absolutely terrified while doing so?"

"Being mature. Sensible. I felt safe with you. I felt looked after. Like I could trust you, rely on you. And you...you did it so competently. And that was hot. I promise you."

He stopped at a red light, which gave him a moment to turn and study her properly. He was sure he looked as confused as he felt. One minute she was calling him needy, and the next she was saying she found him hot?

"Hot?" he repeated, apparently hung up on that word.

She breathed a laugh, but it was her turn to look embarrassed. "A bit."

"A bit?"

She held up a finger and thumb. "A smidgen?"

"Right." He nodded dubiously as the light turned green and he put the car back into gear. "Are you just trying to soothe my toxically fragile masculinity?"

"No. I'm trying to explain why you don't need to pretend to be someone else."

He let out a long breath. "Jules… I have no idea if you're really trying to help me or if this is one of Jay's weird pranks and he's put you up to it, but this is kind of heavy for a car journey. We've only been going forty minutes."

"It's not a prank. And normal conversations are boring, don't you think?"

"But far less likely to cause a complete mental breakdown."

"Right," she said, chastised. "Sorry."

A full thirty seconds of blessed quiet went by, then she said, "I really am trying to help. How about… OK. New idea for a Christmas gift: I wrangle you an invitation to stay for dinner at the Penningtons'. You can have a whole evening to talk to Fel. Or try to."

"God, you're offering to be my charity wingman. Because I don't feel pathetic enough."

It was a shame the car was moving so he couldn't bang his head repeatedly against the steering wheel. Why had he ever thought this road trip might be fun? The Ortons were all hell. Devils in pretty skin.

"Jules, please... If you want to give me something for Christmas, can it please be the gift of silence?"

The irony of William being the one to ask her to stop talking wasn't lost on Jules. If she'd had to predict how a long car journey with William would have gone, it would have been with him talking incessantly and cheerfully of inanities, and with her interjecting increasingly barbed set downs in an effort to shut him up. Probably culminating in her saying something brutal that would have led to several hours of uncomfortable silence.

Instead, she'd jumped straight to the brutality.

Possibly, she reflected, she was out of practice at being helpful. She didn't normally care enough to get involved in other people's problems. Especially not when they were of their own making. The world was stupid. People were stupid. And she was normally happy to merely watch, hiding her contempt behind a mask of indifference.

People often made the mistake of thinking she was shy. She was the girl who sat alone in the corner at parties. Who didn't really speak until spoken to. But she wasn't shy at all. You had to care what people thought of you in order to feel self-conscious. And she honestly didn't care.

Who was she meant to look up to? Her parents? With their toxic relationship and multiple infidelities, their parenting style veering unpredictably between bullying and neglect? Her older sister Jess, in all her selfish, spoilt, temperamental mean-girl glory? Her brother Jay, who hardly noticed who he hurt on his path to self-destruction? Only a few months ago, he had crashed his car *again*. He had nearly died *again*. And did he care what that did to her?

She had very few friends. By choice. Fel was the closest. They'd met at boarding school, Jules preferring books to company and Fel preferring animals. The two weird, loner girls, sharing a space on the sidelines of life, bonding over the things they *didn't* like, rather than the things they did.

But it was still a friendship. It was more important to Jules than she ever openly showed. She might not have found many people worthy of her time, but that didn't mean she didn't get lonely. The party at Deveron would have been the first time she'd seen Fel in months, and she had been stupidly looking forward to it. Then Fel had skipped it, because of her *horse*. So when William appeared in the crowd and his face fell at Fel's absence, it was her own stupid hope and disappointment she saw mirrored there.

She had been angry. So she'd been mean to William. Because it was easier to hate the world than admit it hurt you.

Now she was trying to atone for how she'd spoken to him last night. Hah. What an *excellent* job she was doing of it.

She shifted in her seat, the tension in the car so awkward she would have gladly run. But she was trapped in this mess of her own making, having stirred up an ants' nest when she thought she was only gently prodding a teddy bear, the unbearable sensation of them crawling up her skin.

Sorry, she wanted to say.

Sorry. You're nice. You're too nice.
Fel isn't worth it.
She likes Coldplay. She doesn't read books. She's not the one.

But William was glacially still beside her, making no motion except those necessary to drive the car. Eyes flicking to the rearview mirror, the wing mirror, hand reaching for the gearstick, his jumper sleeve pushed back now the car was warm—too warm, too hot, *suffocating*—the tendons on his lightly freckled wrist corded and tense.

She'd never seen William angry. Hadn't realised he was capable of it.

Was it honestly so terrible that he was always happy and smiling? Why had she needed to destroy that? To bring him down to her level?

He let out a heavy breath, his shoulders rising and falling. It made her stomach turn over, her heart start to pound, waiting for him to speak.

She was a coward.

"Why *are* you trying to help me with Fel?"

By some miracle, or maybe his good upbringing, maybe his inherent good nature, his tone was almost pleasant, conversational.

"You don't like me," he continued. "You can't think I'm worthy of her. And you told me yourself that love, relationships, they're all a self-delusional myth. So why are you trying to help me?"

"Like I said, you're nicer than I thought."

"Nice enough for Fel?"

"She won't date you, Will." Her guilt clearly didn't prevent her from ripping the plaster off. Wasn't that kinder though? In the end? "She doesn't date anyone."

He flinched slightly but forced a light smile. "I see." He glanced at her. "Like you, then."

"Me?"

"Jay once said you never date. That you seem to hate all men. I'm beginning to see what he meant."

She blushed, which was really bloody annoying, because she had nothing to be embarrassed about. "I have dated. I'm not..." *A virgin,* she stopped herself from saying. Partly because she really didn't want to start talking about sex with William Shilstone and partly because it was none of his business. "But I've never met a guy who hasn't been a complete disappointment."

"You're waiting for The One?"

He said it mockingly, but she forgave him. He was entitled to a little spite after what she'd just put him through.

"Not *The Mythical One*, no. They don't exist. Just someone who isn't a complete arsehole."

He gave her an ironic smile. "Someone *nice?*"

"Yes," she said, unashamed. "Someone nice. Someone kind. Someone who doesn't think only with his dick and see relationships as nothing more than a giant pissing contest, just notches on a bedpost."

"Love, then. That's what you're waiting for."

"I don't think it has to be *love* to be treated with a bit of respect."

Will acknowledged her point with a thoughtful expression, absorbing it in silence before glancing at her again, a frown creasing his brow. "Did someone... Did someone treat you disrespectfully, Jules?"

The awkward concern with which he asked made it clear what he really meant. Assault, or worse.

"No. Not any one particular person. I don't have any bad experiences like *that*, thank God." She waved a hand. "It's just a general procession of one loser after another. Or it was. Until I gave up completely."

"When was that? When did you decide?"

"Probably my twentieth birthday party. When my boyfriend copped off with someone else."

"*Copped off*," Will repeated. "Haven't heard that expression in a while."

"It's a good one, don't you think?" she said, not at all put out by this digression into linguistic appreciation.

"It is. But I'm sorry. That guy was clearly terrible."

"They all are."

"And I'm clearly biased, but I don't think that's *entirely* true."

She just shrugged, too relieved to be having a more-or-less civilised conversation with Will to bother pushing the point.

"But that's...nearly four years," he said wonderingly.

"What is?"

"Since you last dated."

"Yeah," she agreed uncomfortably. "I guess it is."

"Don't you miss it?"

"The humiliation and heartbreak?"

"No. I mean the good bits. The...um..."

"If you say 'the physical act of love' I will hit you."

He waggled his eyebrows. "The physical act of love,

Jules," he murmured, voice low. "Don't you miss it?"

Laughing, she smacked his arm. It was firm. Above-averagely so. "I said I don't date, Will. Not that I don't have sex."

"Oh." His eyes went wide, his cheeks went red, and he fell silent, apparently at a loss for words.

Chapter 6

They needed to stop for petrol. Which was fortunate. Because he really needed to stop talking about sex with Jay's little sister.

He grabbed some snacks when he went to pay and handed them to Jules when he got back in the car.

"Tuck in. We'll stop for lunch in an hour or two, but I'd like to get a bit of distance covered first."

They were barely south of Aberdeen. They'd been stuck in slow-moving traffic for ages, a lane closed due to a jackknifed lorry. Roadworks. Christmas-traffic congestion. *Driving home for Christmas...*

He put the Chris Rea song on as they pulled out of the petrol station, laughing at Jules' expression.

"It's a classic!" he protested. "Please tell me you're not Scrooge enough to hate Christmas songs?"

"I'm no Scrooge. I like fun."

"I'm not sure pulling the wings off flies counts. Is Wednesday Adams your spirit guide?"

She smacked his arm again, which he didn't mind at all. For all her spiky attitude, she hit like a butterfly. He laughed, glad beyond expressing that they seemed to have moved past the character assassination stage of the journey.

Their speed picked up too, the traffic improving. It had stopped snowing a while ago, and the road was completely clear, a wet black line cutting through the stark white countryside. Their estimated arrival time at the Penningtons' was currently nine PM.

"Am I allowed to eat these in here?" asked Jules, cautiously opening a packet of crisps. "I don't want to get crumbs on your ludicrous upholstery."

"It gets valeted weekly. Besides, Ben's seen far worse than crumbs."

She pulled a face. "I don't want to ask."

"Probably for the best."

She ate a few crisps, then said, "Jay calls this car the party bus."

"Yes."

"And your yacht, the party boat. And your jet—"

"The party plane? Not very imaginative, is he?"

Jules chuckled. She crunched another crisp. He could smell the salt of them, the oil. When he'd got back into the car at the petrol station, it had been the smell of *her* that filled the car's interior. That woman smell of soap and shampoo and moisturiser. Faint perfume. Soft, clean clothes, and soft, clean hair. Clean, soft skin. He banished a vision of Jules in the shower from his brain.

"Don't you mind though?" she asked.

"Mind what?"

"Always being the one who...um...puts out. Hosting-wise, I mean."

Not this again.

She must have sensed his irritation because she said hastily, "I'm not criticising. Honestly I'm not. It's just... Well... I don't really like people all that much. The idea of throwing a party is alien to me. Why would I go to all that effort just to subject myself to *people*." She shuddered at the thought. "I'm trying to understand it."

"I like people," he answered simply. Truthfully. "I like them to have fun. I like to make people happy."

"I like people to be happy too. If they deserve it."

"Everyone deserves that, Jules."

"No. Not the awful people."

"There are very few truly awful people in the world. Everyone is just...dealing with their own crap, in their own way. Sometimes well, and sometimes poorly, but at their core, I'm sure they're good."

"God." She seemed stunned. "You really *are* nice."

"Most people are."

"No, no." She shook her head. "Now you're just delusional."

"Mmm," he agreed, smiling. "Must be low blood sugar. Could you unwrap me one of those bars?"

She did and passed it to him, her fingers grazing his as he took it without taking his eyes off the road. He chewed and drove, studiously ignoring the tingles the touch of her fingers had left on his palm.

Dean Martin started playing on the car's stereo. *Let it Snow*.

"Now *this* is a Christmas classic," said Jules appreciatively, starting to sing quietly along. Will smiled to himself. He should have known. These gothy alternative girls often had freakishly traditional streaks. He suspected half their cynicism came from the fact the world wasn't the fairytale their hearts desired.

Although, in Jules' case, her jaundiced attitude was easily explained. Her parents. He'd met them several times, but once had been enough. The expression in Jay's eyes when he spoke of them had been enough. They were that rare thing: truly awful people.

He risked a glance at Jules where she sat beside him, singing softly to herself, looking out at the snowy landscape rushing by. No wonder that Chris Rea song hadn't moved her. She was fleeing her own home for the sanctuary of her friend's. Jay was bearing the disapproval of Sophia's mother rather than his own father's loathing. Jess was... Apparently she was shacked up with some doctor. She'd certainly been frequently absent from the usual social circuit.

No one wanted to go home to Rakely House for Christmas.

Maybe it was easy for him to be optimistic about people when he had loving parents, a happy home. Jules had neither, and the sudden wash of sympathy he felt made his chest ache.

"Here," she said.

He glanced from the road. She'd unscrewed the bottle of water he'd bought and was holding it out to him. He took it, drank, passed it back. "Thank you."

She tipped the bottle to her own lips, then nodded at a sign. "Look. Service station in two miles. Can we stop?"

He looked at the dashboard clock. Nearly one. They'd

barely gone half as far as he'd hoped. But... "Sure," he said. "Let's get lunch. Stretch our legs."

When they reached it, the service station car park was slippery, the thin snow having been crushed to treacherous black ice by the wheels of a hundred cars.

"Careful," he warned as they got out of the car.

Jules grimly surveyed the icy ground. She shivered as she buttoned her coat. Will came around the front of the car to walk beside her as they set off, ready to catch her if she slipped.

Which she did, almost immediately.

She swore, but his arm shot out around her waist, his other arm braced on the bonnet of the nearest parked car as he fought to keep them both upright. She stumbled into him, chest to chest, her weight against him, her knee between his thighs, her hair brushing his chin, his throat. Only for a moment.

"Sorry, sorry..." She stepped away hastily. "Didn't see that patch of ice. Look, over there, they've gritted a path..."

She set off towards it without looking back, which was fortunate, because it gave him a moment to collect his wits, to attempt to forget her body pressed against his, the silk touch of her hair, the warmth of her breath glancing across his throat.

Fuck.

Anyone would think he was the one who hadn't dated in years. What a total overreaction to her accidental closeness. The way his heart pounded, his mind buzzing...

He shook his head, set off after her, and promptly slipped arse over tit, falling hard.

"Does it hurt?" Jules asked, grimacing in sympathy as she held a wet tissue to his cheek, trying to clean tiny grains of gravel from the graze.

"Only my pride," William answered, laughing slightly, then wincing at the movement.

They were sitting in a quiet corner of the service station cafe. The staff had given them a first aid box and some water and tissue—the sturdy blue industrial kind. Jules wasn't much of a nurse, but she was trying her best.

"How's my competence doing now?" he asked wryly as she lifted the tissue and examined his cheek. "Still hot?"

She laughed. "It's endearing. The pratfall. This stoic thing you're faking now."

He grunted in disgust.

In truth, she didn't know quite *what* it was, just that nearly falling only to end up crushed against him had left her stupidly flustered. And turning around a moment later just in time to see him hit the ground had made her heart stop with horror.

Now they were sitting unavoidably close on a little padded bench, the kind upholstered with plasticky wipe-clean fabric, at a little plasticky table with no leg room. She was sitting sideways, turned towards him, her knee drawn up and resting almost on his thigh. Her hand was cupping his jaw, the faintest press of new stubble pricking her hot fingers, while her other hand dabbed awkwardly at his grazed cheek, her eyes fiercely focused there, avoiding shifting up to his, because they were far too close.

The hard edge of his jaw felt heavy against her palm. The hot pulse of his throat was inches away. She could feel the edge of his breath on her knuckles. If she moved her thumb, it would brush his lower lip. Not that she wanted to. But it was all very…male. The size and the feel of him. The firm, flat planes of his body against hers when he'd rescued her from falling.

She'd forgotten what it was like. That's why it all felt so intense. It was just the strangeness of the new and unfamiliar. She hadn't been lying exactly when she'd told him that she still had sex since quitting dating. She just hadn't mentioned that the sex was with her own hand. Or, more recently, the toy she'd bought herself in a fit of feminist courage. And horniness.

It had been a while since a man held her. Since the…um…*physical act of love*. Not four years. But nearly eighteen months. Since an awkward and underwhelming one night stand that had reaffirmed her decision to quit men.

That was why touching William made her skin buzz. Just the strangeness of the new.

Her eyes strayed up. Found his regarding her intently.

"Erm. I think that's done." She released him and shifted back, gathering the used tissue into a ball. "I'll go chuck this. I'll order some food too. What would you like?"

He made to stand. "I'll get it."

She waved him back. "No. Sit. Rest."

"Jules, I only slipped over."

"And whacked your head."

"Mostly my palms." He examined them ruefully. They were a stinging shade of red with small grazes on the heels.

"Stay there," she commanded him. "Just tell me what you want."

He looked up at her. Then past her, to the restaurant fronts beyond. Making his choice.

Chapter 7

"Let me guess," said Jules, as the car once again failed to start. "This kind of thing doesn't normally happen to you?"

Will rolled his eyes and tried the ignition again. Absolutely nothing happened. "Ben is normally raring to go. I assure you."

"Please tell me your penis doesn't share a nickname with your car."

"Well, they *are* both ridiculously over-sized..."

"Oh my God." She groaned, dropping her face into her hands.

He grinned, which was a miracle, given his fucking car wouldn't start, it was freezing cold, and he ached all over.

"Must be an electrical fault," he said, trying the starter again without any success. "Let's head back inside. I'll call someone."

They traipsed back—carefully—into the service station, Jules only making four references to him falling over, which seemed restrained for her.

Actually, she'd taken surprisingly good care of him, being gentle with his bruised pride as much as his bruised flesh. She hadn't even laughed when he slipped, but ran straight to his side, helping him up with hands he was sure were shaking. She'd led him inside, spoken to the staff, tended his wounds, fetched his food, and returned to the table with packets of ibuprofen, paracetamol, and two copies of Jack Kerouac's *On The Road* from the bookshop, which she'd set down with a grin, saying, "You need to rest for a bit. So…Book Club time!"

Unexpected kindness after the emotional beating she'd given him.

Maybe she felt guilty. Though she hadn't said anything he hadn't already been thinking. It was just a lot harder to hear from someone else. Someone who was smart enough to be right. And someone who was funny and incredibly pretty and who, his natural masculine ego being what it was, he would have liked to be able to impress.

Hah. Fat chance of that.

They returned to their table and got out their books. He made the call to his breakdown service while she read, then she went to get them coffee while he caught up.

They'd both read the book before. But it didn't matter. It was only to pass the time.

'…the only people for me are the mad ones, the ones who are mad to live, mad to talk, mad to be saved, desirous of everything at the same time, the ones who never yawn or say a commonplace thing, but burn, burn, burn like fabulous yellow roman candles…'

He glanced up from his page as Jules took a drink of her coffee. Her book was in one hand, and when she set her cup down, she wrapped her other hand around the nape of her neck, completely absorbed in what she was reading, her bright grey eyes alive and her lips softly pressed together.

Emotions flickered over her face as she read. She'd changed her hair at some point from a ponytail to a loosely bound mass almost at the top of her head. Probably so she could sit back against the car's headrest without the coiled mass of dark brown hair getting in the way. Now strands escaped haphazardly. Her over-large jumper had slipped from one shoulder, and the thin line of a black vest top—and half-tucked under it, a black bra strap—were pressing lightly into her smooth skin.

She absently ran her thumb under the strap as she read, adjusting how it lay.

Will dragged his eyes back to his book and read the same line four times in a row, heeding none of it.

It was too noisy to concentrate, anyway. The service station was crowded, the jumble of surrounding conversations a din, and, over it all, a Michael Bublé Christmas song for the millionth time in a row. Jules was right. The original version was better.

He would rather have been sitting with Jules somewhere more comfortable. A hotel lobby, maybe, with plush, comfortable seats and only the faintest murmur of background voices. Real greenery gracing the walls, the caressing heat of a real fire nearby. But the only hotel within walking distance was a Travel Lodge, which wouldn't have been much of an improvement on their current surroundings.

It would be nice, though, to be relaxing at a hotel rather than facing an eight-hour drive. Probably longer, given their luck so far. At this rate, it would be gone midnight by the time they reached the Penningtons' house. No chance of being invited in for dinner. Fel probably wouldn't even come to the door. It would be one of her brothers or sisters—there were six siblings altogether. Jules would slip inside, the door would close in his face, and he'd still have an almost three-hour drive to his parents' house. In the dark and alone.

He looked back at his book.

'A pain stabbed my heart, as it did every time I saw a girl I loved who was going the opposite direction in this too-big world.'

Even Jack seemed to think Fel was a hopeless case.

It took nearly two hours for William's breakdown recovery service to arrive and get his car going again. Jules guessed that was the problem of having such a fancy car. There weren't many people who knew how to fix it.

She'd drunk too much coffee while they waited, too aware of William sitting silent at her side. How boring he must find her, the girl who would sit in silence with a book, when he lived and breathed for parties and company. She'd only bought *On the Road* as a joke, but he'd picked it up and started to read it, as though her weirdness was totally expected, and he was too polite to protest it.

So she had picked up her book too. And anyway. She hadn't quite known what to say to him. All her thoughts kept circling back to Fel. It was under her skin now, this annoying urge to free his heart, make him see sense, set him on the path to some more realistic chance of happiness. Because there were surely plenty of girls in the world who'd be simply ecstatic to have a smart and funny and nice and possibly *above*-averagely attractive man drive eight hundred miles just for the chance of glimpsing their face.

Fel wasn't one of them.

It's not like Jules was *romantic*. She didn't feel she was playing Cupid—or rather, Cupid's medic: the one who followed Cupid around dislodging arrows that had hit the wrong mark. It was just really *annoying* watching William moon over the wrong person. Like watching a moth bump moronically against a light bulb.

She wanted to swot him down. Or cup him in her hands and redirect him. Or something.

Anyway. She was jittery and over-caffeinated when they finally left the service station, and she launched into a lengthy rant about the difficulties of getting a foot in the door of the British publishing industry, mainly to block her mouth from saying anything else.

The car had cooled back down to freezing while it was parked. William jacked the heating up. Too high. She dragged her jumper off and threw it in the back, twisting back around to find William shooting her a glance—his eyes darting to her cleavage then snapping back to the road.

She suppressed a smile.

"Erm... That's what you want to do, is it?" he asked. "Work in publishing?"

As she'd just spent the last twenty minutes telling him

so, this seemed a stupid question. But she answered politely. "Yes, I'd like to be an editor." She dragged the elastic hair tie free from her bun as she spoke. Her jumper had snagged on it, and her bun was rapidly unravelling. "That's the dream, anyway."

Or that's what she attempted to say, but she was holding the elasticated band in her mouth as she spoke, using both her hands to gather her hair. William took her by surprise, reaching out and snagging it from between her lips to hold it for her, his other hand steady on the steering wheel.

"Er. Thanks."

There was a tingle on her lip from where the band had caught against her teeth and stretched tight before gently snapping loose. A tingle from where William's thumb had left the ghost of a touch.

"I believe you were saying *'mmmmf fffmph phmf*'?" he prompted.

"I was *saying* editing is my dream job. Editing fiction."

She finished wrestling her hair into place. Holding it gathered with one hand, she took the hair tie back and secured it. William glanced over. "Not writing?"

"No. I'm not sure I have that urge. Not in any focused way. On my course, it was the analytical stuff I really liked. Pulling the stories apart, seeing how they worked."

"Pulling the wings off flies," he observed musingly. It sounded strangely fond.

"Quite." Then, going out on a limb, "What about you?"

"Me?"

"The surprisingly bookish William Shilstone. Do you write?"

He shook his head. "No. Well..."

"Well...?"

"I used to," he admitted to her avid excitement. "A long, long time ago. I'd actually forgotten all about it until I saw your book this morning at breakfast. I couldn't work out if it was meant to be horror or fantasy. That's what I used to write. Fantasy. Though not the kind your book's about, I don't think. The old-fashioned stuff—Tolkien, Jordan, Sanderson... Epic quests and lots of travelling around riding horses."

"The real nerd stuff, huh?" was what she said, when what she really wanted to say was, *"Oh my God, that is so cool! I love that sort of thing!"* But she was attempting, probably futilely, to cling to the last remnants of her cool-girl veneer. If she had ever possessed such a thing.

"And you don't write anymore? Why did you stop?"

"It was terrible trash. Total juvenile nonsense."

"Well, they *do* say write what you know..."

He huffed a breath of laughter. "Excellent burn. Ten out of ten."

She sketched a bow as best she could whilst wearing a seat belt. "Thank you."

"Thinking about it," he continued, "I don't think it was the sword fights or even the magic that drew me to those sorts of stories. I think it was the idea of travelling around with a group of friends, having adventures, meeting new people along the way."

"Maybe that's what you should write."

"And the romance," he blurted, as though he had to follow this trail of thought to the end. "There was always a romance. Some elf queen or faerie princess..."

"Oh my God. It's Fel." She stared at the side of his face, his suddenly tense jaw, the flush on his cheeks. "That's what Fel is to you. She's your elf queen, riding around on horseback, totally mysterious and unknown."

He said nothing.

She wanted to mock. Of course she did. She wanted to laugh and crow and tease him forever. Instead she said, as seriously as she could manage, "You know she's just a real human girl, right? Snores. Picks her feet."

He flashed her a look. "Does she?"

"No. Or probably not. She really is basically an angel. *But*...she did once talk to me for an hour about the life cycle of some kind of equine intestinal parasite."

William shrugged. "I could live with that."

"Mm. Zoning out. Staring into her big brown eyes, seeing the answers to the universe held there, the echo of your soul..."

He shrugged again, as though that was entirely feasible.

Disgruntled, Jules shifted in her seat, moving the seatbelt from where it was digging into her neck. "You've never even spoken to her."

"I know."

"I don't understand it. But I'm not romantic. I guess I never will understand."

"Have you never had that feeling? You catch sight of someone and the world just stops?"

"Time stands still?" she added sarcastically. But he nodded.

"You see this person and they are just *perfection*. Like no one else you've ever seen. And you'd rearrange your entire life just for the chance to get to know them..."

He trailed off, seeming to recollect where he was, who he was talking to. That he was actually saying this nonsense out loud. He scrubbed a hand over the back of his neck, then focused very intently on overtaking a car Jules was fairly sure he didn't need to overtake.

"This poetical stuff is all very well," she commented when they'd settled back into their lane. "But you've spent years shagging your way around the globe just like my brother and all your other friends—"

"Not *that* much shagging—"

"It's not like you've been saving yourself for your one true love."

He laughed. "This isn't *actually* some medieval fairy story. I have a mad crush, Jules. But I'm not insane."

"So even love isn't enough to keep men from straying."

She blurted it out much the same way as he had made his confession about romance. As though it was the inevitable end of everything they had been saying. Because, really, that was at the heart of her fears. That all men would be like her father. Affair after affair. You could give your heart to someone, but how could you ever guarantee they wouldn't break it? Wouldn't just toss it aside when they got bored or a new pretty face came along?

He must have heard something in her voice. The betraying edge of sorrow. Or maybe it was just that she was clearly mad and in need of careful handling. Because he gave her the longest look he could spare from the road and said, very, very gently, "That's a bit of a stretch, Jules. I'm not saying I'm in love with Fel. If I was...of course I wouldn't be with anyone else. I don't condone cheating. And neither do my friends. We might...erm...be more familiar with casual sorts of situations, but there's definitely a line. Not all men cheat."

Jules said nothing, too embarrassed and raw to come up with the right words. She folded her arms and watched the dark countryside pass. Night had already fallen, and it was barely five.

"So you don't...?" she said eventually, her voice unusually small. "You don't love her?"

"No," William said carefully, as though he was testing the truth of the word. "No. I don't think so. But I think I could, if I got to know her."

Chapter 8

This journey wasn't boring, Will could say that much. But it *was* taking a long time. They'd covered more ground metaphorically than they had literally.

It was almost seven PM when they got far enough down the M1 for signs to York to appear.

Jules was quiet at his side. Had been for some time. Her head was turned away, looking out through the passenger-side window. Or maybe she was asleep. It was hard to tell in the dull muddy orange of the motorway's streetlamps.

He hoped she *was* asleep. That she wouldn't wake until they were south of York. On a deep, instinctive level, he knew that any reminder of her home, her parents, would cause her pain. Especially at this time of year, when all those deepest threads of one's soul were pulled tight.

Christmas was a time for family, wasn't it? For home comforts. None of that to be found at Rakely.

The sense of brotherly protectiveness he'd felt at the start of their journey surged back, stronger than before. Jules *would* spend Christmas with the Penningtons, having a nice time, being appreciated and cared for and made welcome, just the way she deserved. He would make sure she got there, no matter what.

But Jules stirred and sat up. "We're not going to get to Fel's until well after midnight, are we? Why don't you drop me here at Rakely? I can get the train from York tomorrow."

He shook his head. "No. No. It's fine. I'm driving anyway. I may as well have company." He shot her a reassuring smile she probably couldn't see in the dim light.

"But Fel's place in Kent must be another three hours or so past Herlingcote. And then you'll have to drive back. That's an extra six hours, Will. And you've been driving all day. You must be exhausted."

"It's fine."

"I know you want to see Fel, but..."

He said nothing, his mind filling in the words she didn't say. *But this is mad. But she'll be asleep. But there's no point.*

"How about..." he said, turning over possibilities in his mind. "Maybe we do break the journey. But not at Rakely. There's a hotel not far past York. I stay there sometimes when I'm visiting Jay, or doing long drives like this. They might not have any rooms at such short notice, but we should at least be able to get dinner. It'll give me a rest. Then I'll be fine to drive the rest of the way."

He felt, rather than saw, her frowning uncertainty.

"It's not safe to drive when you're tired. I think we really should stop overnight somewhere. I'll just let Fel know I won't be there until tomorrow."

"OK," he agreed. He had been looking forward to seeing his parents, but Jules was right. It would practically be tomorrow morning by the time he got there anyway. "I doubt they'll have rooms, but I'm sure we can find somewhere that does."

She seemed happy enough with that and got out her phone, probably to text Fel. The bright little screen was in the corner of his eye as he drove, Fel on the other end of it.

If they arrived tomorrow, in the daytime, he'd have a much better chance of seeing her. Maybe they'd ask him to stay for lunch. And he could... He could...

Stare?

He tried to imagine it. Sitting in the kitchen or the dining room at Fraversham—he'd never visited the house, but these big old country houses were all more or less the same. Sitting next to Fel, her brown eyes on his as he said...

What? What did you say to the girl you'd spent eight years idolising?

Something about intestinal parasites apparently. He laughed to himself at the thought, aware of the glance Jules gave him, though she didn't question why he was smiling.

Or maybe he'd talk about faeries and elves. Maybe something about thunderbolts and time standing still.

It was all absurd, wasn't it? Nothing he could imagine seemed remotely realistic.

"That's what Fel is to you. She's your elf queen..."

Not quite. Jules was exaggerating, as usual. Many of his thoughts about Fel were extremely...um...base and ignoble. But when he'd heard himself say, *"You see this person and they are just perfection. Like no one else you've ever seen..."* it had felt almost as though he was hearing someone else, watching a performance. Fine words, but oddly distant from him. Hollow. Maybe some things felt more true when you voiced them out loud. And maybe others rang false.

Fel was just a girl. And he fancied her. No mystery to it, no real romance. Perhaps not even any real *feelings*, if he forced himself to stop and think about it.

An image came into his mind as clear as day—as often used to happen when he was writing his stories, all those years ago. This image was of a young man, a sailor, a submariner in fact. It was the nineteen-forties. Wartime. He had a tiny, narrow bunk, and there was a creased and faded photograph stuck to the wall near his pillow, the corners dogeared. It was a picture of a beautiful girl, her white teeth the brightest thing in the whole bunk room. But on closer inspection, it wasn't a true photograph, but a page torn from a magazine. The girl wasn't *his* girl from back home. She was an actress, completely unknown to him. Just a totem, a symbol, a placeholder for a longing that had no home…

God. It felt so real. So true. He itched to write it, even as he recognised the truth it was trying to tell him.

Years and years of casual hookups and relationships lasting a month or two at most, all of it empty, him feeling no connection to any of those girls. But it had been OK, he'd reassured himself, because his heart was already engaged. He was just biding his time, treading water, until he got his chance with Fel.

But had it been an excuse? The comfort blanket he held onto like a lost child because it was easier than admitting he was bloody lonely and he was desperate to connect, truly connect, with another soul?

What would that be like, to find someone who loved every inch of you as deeply as you loved every inch of them? Who you could talk to for hours? Who was your best friend and lover all in one? Someone as funny and fun as any of his friends, but who he fancied madly, and who fancied him just as madly in return…

Beside him, Jules stretched and sat up, spotting an illuminated sign on the turning they'd just taken. The hotel was only a mile away.

"Thank God," she said. "We're almost there."

Chapter 9

THE HOTEL WAS OFFENSIVELY picturesque. Jules could tell, even in the dark of a winter's night, because it was illuminated by yellow-gold Christmas lights strung under every eave and around every window. Probably early Victorian, made of weathered York stone, with red Virginia creeper growing up the walls, mingled ivy streaking it with green. Or those would have been the colours in daylight. Lit the way it was, it was shades of sable and silvered ebony.

There was an enormous evergreen tree in the circle of lawn before the house. It was decorated for Christmas, of course, a million tiny points of light among the shadowed boughs like heaven brought to earth. The gravel driveway curved around it, the old carriage turning circle. William stopped the car before the steps to the broad front porch, and a suited valet came forward to take the keys.

An offensively *expensive* hotel. But this was William Shilstone. What else had she expected?

The woman on reception looked covertly panicked as she tried to conjure a restaurant table on the night before Christmas Eve at zero notice. But the moment William had given his name, her slightly dubious welcome had transformed into vibrant, efficient courtesy. William, to give him credit, seemed more or less oblivious to the effect he was having and merely stood politely waiting, flashing Jules a reassuring smile.

For her part, she might have wished she was less travel-crumpled and knackered-looking, her hair beyond a disaster, but she didn't much care that she was wearing biker boots and an ancient jumper in the midst of all this polished wood and tasteful, understated finery. Her family might not have even a quarter of the Shilstone's wealth, but her father was a viscount and she'd grown up at Rakely House. She was as used to these sorts of surroundings as William.

Even if her budget seldom stretched to them.

"I think we can fit you into the bar room," the receptionist said with a hint of apology. "If that would be acceptable?"

"That sounds perfect," William replied.

And it really was. A low table, squishy leather chairs, a quiet corner by the roaring log fire. Jules suspected the table was only free because the fire was ferociously hot, but she didn't mind at all. She stripped off her jumper and held her hands out to the flames. After the dark monotony of the motorway, the bright flames were a beacon of cosy welcome.

She settled back into the soft leather armchair with an audible sigh of appreciation. William's car was extremely comfortable, but after hours in the same seat, she was stiff, her back aching. God only knew how he was feeling after falling on the ice. She looked over and found him watching her.

Self-conscious, she sat up. Maybe she *was* making herself a little too comfortable for a hotel like this.

She picked up the menu from the table, and William followed suit. He had removed his jumper too, revealing his white t-shirt, and forcing her to acknowledge that his arms were, perhaps, above-averagely nice. Distractingly so.

"I'm starving," he murmured, studying the menu.

"Mm," she agreed, dragging her eyes back to her own. But when she looked up, he was again looking at her.

"I know what I want," he said. "Do you?"

"Hmm..." She ran a finger across her bottom lip, back and forth, her devilish side coming out to play. "Hmm... Maybe something big. And hot. And filling."

She met his eyes, trying not to laugh as his look narrowed, unamused. She gave up the attempt, and let her laugh break free even as she innocently protested, "What? Why are you looking at me like that?"

"Because I didn't realise you were twelve."

"What? I just meant the roast. Some juicy meat. Maybe pork? Toad in the hole? Spotted d—"

He snatched the menu out of her hand and waved over a waitress, muttering some threat about getting her the children's menu. But his cheeks were pink, and he looked everywhere but at her until the waitress had left.

Biting back the temptation to tease him further—or at least, in that particular way—she settled loftily in her chair, legs crossed, elbows on the armrests, fingers steepled under her chin. In a deep, overly formal voice, she said, "So,

William. Tell me what it is that you do?"

He gave her a questioning look, suspicious again. "Do?"

She shrugged, then continued in her normal voice, "I've yacked on at you about my career hopes and dreams. But I have no idea what yours are."

"Um..." He scrubbed the back of his neck, inadvertently flexing his bicep in an irritating manner. "I'm not sure I have any."

"Your dad does something businessy, doesn't he?"

"He did. He retired a couple of years ago."

"And your mum does...something. Something somethingy."

He smiled slightly. "Yes. *Something somethingy* in the City. But she's retired too now."

"Obviously, I know you don't need to work..."

"No," he agreed, looking embarrassed by the fact.

"So it's just parties and fun, forever?"

He shrugged. "That's basically what my dad told me to do. He worked crazily hard, and so did my mum. And their parents, and their parents..."

His dad was a baron, she knew. William would inherit the title one day. But the family's fortune had mostly been created toward the end of the nineteenth century. She had a few horrible old relatives who still sniffed and talked about *new* money.

"He said he didn't want that life for me. That I ought to 'enjoy the fruits of his labour'. That I ought to...have a life where I'd be able to make time for my own family. Whenever they came along. But he always did, anyway. Have time for me, I mean. My mum too. No matter how busy they were."

"Came to watch your school nativity plays, that sort of thing?"

"Yes," he admitted, and the look he gave her held a trace of guilt, as though he knew she would inevitably be comparing his good fortune to her own. Or lack thereof.

A waiter arrived with their drinks. William thanked him as he set the glasses on the table. Jules picked up her wine. "What about writing? You could give that another go."

"What would I write about? I've done nothing interesting."

"Fiction doesn't have to be true."

"But it needs to mean something, doesn't it?"

"I don't think it needs to *mean* anything. Just...*feel* like something."

"I've spent years trying to pretend I don't have feelings. Or not those poetical sorts."

She smiled dryly. "The girly kind?"

His answering smile was just as dryly self-aware. "Yes. All those finer feelings. They're all dead and shrivelled up. I've flushed them out of my system with radioactive masculinity."

"And beer."

He lifted his glass in salutation of her point. "Basically one and the same."

"Kerouac drank. And slept around. And he wrote the rawest kind of poetry."

"Probably when he *was* drunk. Or worse."

There was a pause while they both sipped their drinks. William put his pint glass down square on the beer mat, keeping his fingers wrapped around it, hesitating a moment before looking up. "We've never really done this before, have we?"

"This?"

"Talking. Civil conversation. Or more or less civil." He sat back in his chair, giving her a smile, an elbow on the chair's armrest, long, clever fingers curving lightly over the leather edge. "At Rakely, you're normally in your room, avoiding us all. And at parties and things…you do that thing you do."

"Which thing?"

He laughed, gesturing to her face with those same clever fingers. "The thing you're doing now. Scowling and dark looks. Making it clear you don't want to be there. And you definitely don't want to talk to anyone."

"That's because I don't."

"But why not?"

"Because people are idiots."

"Maybe compared to you. I guess that's the problem with being the smartest person in the room."

She stared at him for a moment, sure he must be taking the piss. But he didn't smirk or do anything, other than look vaguely embarrassed and reach for his drink. She watched the movement, his arm, his hand, the skin dusted with faint freckles, the hair on his forearm limned with gold from the firelight.

"No, no," she said lightly, trying to brush it off. "I'm pretty sure it's everyone else that's the problem."

He chuckled. "Of course."

It was far more awkward to speak to him like this. With

him not driving, but able to sit there and study her. Meet her eyes properly. Deeply.

All their words felt more real. They hung in the warm, still air, along with the scent of gravy and ale and woodsmoke. Muggy, ancient, medieval scents. Permanent and lasting. No speeding motorway to whip her words away and leave them safely behind. Just Will, watching her speak, his eyes now able to challenge hers. Hold her gaze and test it.

She got out her phone, needing another way to escape. She sent a pointless message to Fel. *At hotel. Have ordered roast.*

~~*At hotel. With man who worships you.*~~

Their food arrived. They ate without speaking for a few moments other than to say things like, "This looks good," and, "Better than the service station." Then William did that thing he did. The thing where he worked out exactly what a person needed, and how to make sure they were enjoying themselves. He talked to her about books. He talked to her about food, and boring things, the weather and Christmas and what they had bought for whom. Except none of it was boring, because he was too funny and full of good-humoured wit to ever be that. And because he smiled those smiles he had, the ones that were just so irresistibly nice. And he listened to her as though all the stupid things she said were really actually incredibly interesting.

She could imagine him anywhere in the world, a bar, a beach, a mountain track; he'd strike up conversation with anyone just as easily and affably as he spoke to her now.

"Is this a Christmas miracle?" he asked when the waitress had taken away their plates.

"Is what?"

"We've been talking for an hour. And you didn't seem to hate it."

"I knew it was some kind of trick. You, keeping me talking by acting all interesting and stuff, just to prove a point."

He chuckled. "No, Jules. I really am '*all interesting and stuff*'. That was one-hundred percent just me being me. We've had what I believe the experts call A Completely Normal Conversation." He skewered her with a grin. "Admit it though. It wasn't terrible."

"That's different."

"Why?"

Because it's you, she almost said, before mentally back-pedalling in horror. "Because you've turned out not to be a complete idiot."

"High praise."

"It is from me."

"I know."

He said it with his eyes on hers, amused and warm. Blue and honest and open. Inviting her to look, as though they were a window onto a sunny field. Somewhere she could stand and stare her fill, maybe even climb through, walk into the flower meadow hand-in-hand—

She snapped her eyes away. Looked suspiciously at her wine glass. Was she drunk?

He leant forwards in his chair, elbows on his knees, a teasing smile on his boyish, handsome face. "It's not a crime, you know," he said in a faux-whisper, glancing around the room, pretending to check they weren't being overheard. "It's OK to enjoy someone's company."

They were sitting close enough to touch. Her boots had long been abandoned, a pile of empty leather and metal discarded under the table. She didn't care about sitting in a luxury hotel in her worn, old socks. They had paid, hadn't they? Who cared what anyone wore?

Those were the thoughts that roared like wind through her mind as she watched herself lift one socked foot, place the ball of it against the bone and muscle of William's knee, the edge of his thigh, and shove, that teasing smile still on his face, the scowl still on hers, their eyes locked.

"I think it is, when the company's yours."

He chuckled, made a grab for her foot. She snatched it back and tucked it safely under her on the chair. The change in posture made her sit forwards, made it impossible to miss the way Will's eyes dipped to the front of her vest, the rather shameless amount of skin visible above the tight black fabric.

Hah.

Men.

Except her scoff was accompanied by something smug and pleased. By something hot, a twist of excitement low in her gut. By a vision, swiftly following, of Will's head, warm lips brushing the sensitive skin, the upper swell of her breasts, her fingers running up the back of his neck, over the short hairs at his nape to the longer, thicker hair on top, holding him there as their breathing turned ragged and he pulled the front of her vest down—

Oh shit.

No, no, no, no. She couldn't like him. Not *Biffy*.

Not the crowd-following, people-pleasing sheep. Not the man who threw ridiculous parties—parties with live zebras, for fuck's sake. Who hung around with shaggers and rogues, with people who went through women like it was a competitive sport.

She *had* to dislike him. For the sake of her sanity.

And because *he*...he liked her best friend.

Chapter 10

WILL MUFFLED A YAWN with the back of his hand. It was gone ten, and they were still in their corner by the fire, Jules staring into the glowing embers.

He'd only had one drink in case they couldn't get rooms here and he needed to drive them somewhere else, but he was drowsy with heat and food. The fire was crackling softly. There was the mellow background hum of their fellow guests' voices and the faint sound of a piano coming from the dining room beyond the bar.

Winter evergreens shrouded the fire's mantel, tiny golden lights scattered within, like Christmas fireflies. The air smelt of pine and leather and warmth. Of whisky and ale and women's perfume. Jules was quiet. Tired too, he guessed. Her cheek rested on one hand. Her shoulders were bare cream. Her dark hair and flashing eyes were chocolate and silver.

It was all so damn lovely it hurt.

There were moments you wanted to live inside forever. Some passed by so quickly you only realised looking back just how special they were. And others cocooned you. Let you watch, and know, and appreciate every minute.

This was one of those. A perfect evening. Even though he ached and wasn't remotely in the place he had intended to be. Even though he'd spent the day being abused by Jay's kid sister, sat in a car, stuck in traffic, stuck in a service station for more hours than he cared to remember.

Somehow, he'd enjoyed it all.

"Anything else I can get you?"

The waiter stood by their table, collecting empty glasses. William met Jules' eyes. "I think we'd better go see if there's any room at the inn."

She nodded in agreement, so he told the waiter no thanks. They stood up. Jules stretched. The movement arched her back, lifting her breasts.

That bloody vest top. Nothing but tiny straps and tight, elastic stretch.

God. It was like he'd never seen breasts before. It had been bad enough on the road, being forced to look at the grimy tailgate of some lorry when she was sitting *right there*, that banquet sight an impossible glance away. But to have her sitting across from him, leaning forwards in her chair...

Jay's sister, he reminded himself. Get a grip.

They went back out into the hotel lobby. He smiled one of his most winning smiles at the poor lady on reception. She was regarding his optimistic approach with a sinking sort of look.

"Good evening. I don't suppose you happen to have two rooms for tonight?"

"Two?" she repeated, before masking her dismay with a coolly efficient smile. "I'll just check for you, sir."

She tapped on her keyboard. It may as well have been just for show. Surely they were fully booked.

"I know it's terribly short notice," he said apologetically.

"But you wouldn't force a pregnant lady out into the cold. Not at Christmas?" Jules stood close by his shoulder, looking round-eyed at the receptionist, hand on her stomach.

He shook his head in disbelief. Bloody Ortons. "Ignore her," he told the stricken receptionist. He nudged Jules with his knee. "That baby is nothing but roast beef and sticky toffee pudding."

She nudged him back. With her hip. The curve of it against his thigh. "Excuse me. It was steamed banoffee. I can't believe you've forgotten the make-up of our very own baby."

"That baby's between you and the kitchen. I had no part in it."

She smirked at him, biting her lip. "Pity."

For the love of all things holy.

He wrenched his attention back to the receptionist. Why did he always have to blush like a bloody schoolboy?

The woman was still clicking around on her computer. Jules' hip was still brushing his. But he ignored that.

He also completely failed to move away. But he ignored that too.

The receptionist's frown foretold bad news. Then she suddenly brightened, looking up. "Oh! We've had a cancellation come through due to the weather. But I'm afraid it's only one room. A double." She glanced from him to Jules. The receptionist probably thought they were a couple. He flushed sightly, standing back, straightening away from Jules, worried that maybe their close body-language was—

"We'll take it!" announced Jules.

He shot her a look. She was practically vibrating with excitement, her eyes glowing. At the thought of...sharing a double with him?

"Erm..." he said.

"Please, please!" she insisted, grabbing his arm. "Please. Let it be your Christmas present to me. You *have* to do this."

He'd never seen anyone look so excited about anything in his life. And he had absolutely no idea why. It surely wasn't the thought of...

He cleared his throat and nodded at the receptionist. "Thank you. We'll take it."

Will followed Jules warily into the room. She walked into the centre of the space, hands held out as she turned an ecstatic circle.

"One bed trope!" she exclaimed. "I can't believe it's happening for real."

"One bed what?"

"Come on, literature boy. You know what a trope is."

"A recurrent theme or motif?"

She nodded, sitting down on the bed with an experimental bounce. He supposed that was almost a trope itself. Something everybody always did when they first walked into a hotel room.

"You don't know the genre, but there's this thing that always happens. Two people get to a hotel, or a cabin, or wherever they're stuck for the night, and there is Only. One. Bed."

"Right," he said, beginning to understand the idea. But not why she was so excited about experiencing it. With him.

His eyes strayed to the bed. To Jules on the bed. To that bloody vest top.

"And these two people," he asked, affecting a neutral tone. "They sleep in the bed together?"

"Well, one of them always insists on sleeping on the floor or something."

"I'm not sleeping on the floor."

"I know. I'm not talking about *us*." She waved a dismissive hand. "This is just in stories."

"Yes. But. Here we really are. Actually with only one bed."

She looked down as though only just realising what she was sitting on. When she looked up, her cheeks were pink.

Hah.

Maybe he could get some revenge for all the teasing downstairs. For the whole day.

He strolled over to the window, taking a deliberately casual glance out. "And these two people," he said, turning back to stand with his arms folded, leaning against the wall. "Who get stuck together for the night sharing a bed, are they attracted to each other?"

"Yes."

"But they're not together?"

"No. They...they normally pretend not to be attracted to each other."

"And I suppose they're trying to fight this extremely deep, intense, physical attraction for..." He mimicked her casual hand wave. "For reasons."

"Um. Yes."

"So, they lie there all night, close together, not touching but desperate for each other?"

"Yes..."

"I think I get it. It's a sexual tension thing. Will they, won't they...? That sort of thing?"

She swallowed. Nodded.

"Well. Excellent!" He clapped his hands together breezily. "We'll be fine then. Because we're absolutely not attracted to each other at all, right?"

He laughed at the look on her face. Oh, it felt *good* to be the one winding her up for a change. *Little Miss Something Hot and Filling* indeed. Bloody Ortons. All devils.

There was a knock on the door. The porter with their bags. When Will returned, Jules was still sitting on the bed, frowning.

Chapter 11

Jules had underestimated the awkwardness of a real Only One Bed situation. William was completely correct. Here they really were, actually with only one bed. And the knowing way he met her eyes while talking about sexual tension ramped up her own tension a million-fold. Her bicep-ogling downstairs clearly hadn't been as subtle as she thought.

She hopped off the bed as he set their bags down in a corner of the room.

"You know I only agreed to the room for the laugh of it? It's just a...um...literary appreciation thing?"

He smiled his normal smile, not the alarmingly wicked one from moments before. "I know, Jules. Don't worry. I'm honestly not reading anything into this."

She could only nod. Then she busied herself getting ready for sleep, having to dump half her bag's contents on the bed to find her toothbrush and pyjamas. She went into the bathroom, absolutely refusing to feel awkward or embarrassed. Even if she did linger for much longer than she needed to.

When she came back out, Will was sitting on the bed

reading her book.

Not the Jack Kerouac, but the *other* book. The one from breakfast. She must have taken it out of her bag and left it on the bed.

She squawked and grabbed it from him.

"It's a romance!" he announced, absolutely delighted. "I couldn't work it out from the cover with the bleeding feathers and all. But it's a romance book."

"No. It's not. It's fantasy."

"No, no, give it back. Here, I'll show you..." He held his hand out as though seriously expecting her to hand it over. "Jules. I just want to find the bit I was reading."

"It's a fantasy," she insisted. "It has sword fights."

"But the bit with the guy, the prince, he's on his knees before the girl and he says—"

Her cheeks burnt even harder. She knew exactly what the prince said. It was imprinted on her brain from the five times she'd read it.

"It's a fantasy," she gritted out.

"And then later on—I flicked ahead a bit—there's this absolutely filthy bit where he has her up against the wall and he..." William trailed off at the expression on her face. "Sure. No. It's a fantasy book."

His capitulation was marred by the fact he was biting his lip, trying not to laugh. "Can I borrow it when you've finished?" he asked, eyes gleaming. "Swords and sex. It sounds right up my street."

"Here." She shoved it back at him, smacking it on his chest. "Read it. Laugh. Whatever."

"Come on," he pleaded, turning more serious as she

stomped around to the other side of the bed and busied herself finding a socket for her phone charger. "I'm not laughing *at* you. I've already admitted I used to write far worse stuff. It's just... You're so anti-romance... I was surprised, that's all."

"It's a book. Not real life."

"You can read what you like, Jules. Anyway, I'm not even joking. This really does sound right up my street." He turned the book over and started reading the blurb on the back.

"Then read it if you want to," she said with a sigh, the storm of her embarrassment fading to something only mildly nauseous. She watched him finish reading the blurb and flick to the first page. "I've already read it. So keep it. It's yours. Another Christmas present from me. Sorry it's not wrapped. It is ridiculously raunchy though, so I hope that makes up for it."

He chuckled. "No complaints from me."

She just shook her head, trying to leave the last of her embarrassment behind her. So William Shilstone knew she enjoyed stories about handsome dark princes going nuts for just one girl. So what. Look at him, going nuts for Fel. At least she understood the difference between fantasy and reality.

Will took his turn in the bathroom. The shower started running. Which meant Will was naked in there. And that was something she wasn't at all going to think about. Not even a little bit.

She got two bottles of water from the minibar and put one on each of their bedside tables. Then she sat on the edge of the bed, too self-conscious to get in. It would feel weird to be lying there, all tucked in, with Will wandering around the room. Will climbing in beside her.

He came out of the bathroom.

He was only in boxer shorts.

Jesus fucking Christ. He really didn't get the One Bed trope at all, did he? He was meant to insist on staying dressed, rant and rave at the receptionist for another room, angrily throw himself onto the floor with nothing but a blanket and his seething ill-repressed lust. Instead he stood there, looking all...

Jesus fucking Christ.

"Don't laugh," he said, trying to brazen it out. But his insouciant smile was at odds with the blush in his cheeks, the way he didn't quite meet her eye, but busied himself getting his phone, finding his charger. "I've been in that t-shirt all day. It's gross. And I didn't plan on an overnight stay, so I only have one spare for tomorrow. I promise I'm not trying to seduce you with my manly physique."

She cleared her throat. "Suspiciously defined for a bookish guy, Will."

He huffed a laugh, unscrewing the lid of his water. "I haven't been bookish in a long time."

How he managed to make that sound dirty, she had no idea.

"And I have friends who look like Hugo Blackton," he continued after a drink of water, giving a shrug. "It's hard not to feel the peer pressure. Hard not to try to keep up."

She opened her mouth, then shut it hastily before she could say something like, *"I don't think you need to worry."*

But she couldn't quite think what else to say. All her higher brain functions were occupied with aesthetic matters, her gaze helplessly tracking over William's bare skin as he crossed back to the bathroom to turn off the light. He was subtly, gently defined. No harsh ridges and snaking veins, but rather the beautiful dips and firm lines left in sand by a retreating tide, his skin as lightly golden.

A new world inviting her to explore.

"No PJs?" she asked, her disaffected tone a lie.

"No. Sorry."

"I could lend you a top."

He laughed, walking back to the bed. "That tiny vest?"

"It'd keep you decent."

"Jules. There's nothing decent about that vest."

She looked away to hide her blush, even as a pleased sort of heat unfurled in her stomach. Will reached down to plug in his charger by the side of the bed, and her eyes inevitably travelled back towards him.

Then she saw the bruises on his shoulder and elbow. She was scrambling across the bed and reaching for him before she knew it.

"Is this from when you fell on the ice?"

He gave the bruises an embarrassed glance. "Er, yeah. It's fine."

"Will..." She touched his arm, just below his elbow. Just below the fresh red bruise.

That was a mistake.

He went absolutely still at the contact. So did she. As though the low, throbbing ebb of tension that had been swirling around them all night had now found its mark.

Pounced. Caught them in its teeth and held them fast.

He was so close. So very male, his frame so much larger than hers. Taut, firm skin and body heat... A caging wall of promise, of sweeping sensation just one touch away...

What would it be like to kiss him? Her hand moving up his arm to the back of his neck, his skin hot against her fingers, his hair cool. His mouth meeting hers and that first taste, mint from his toothpaste, but under that, the secret taste of another person, a hint of iron and sweetness, more a feeling than a flavour, the slide of his tongue drowning her thoughts...

She looked up, met his eyes. In the very same moment he sucked in a breath and stepped back.

But he must feel it too, her mind insisted wildly for one bewildered moment. Surely he felt it too, this tension between them? Because it was alive, and pulsing, and it could only possibly exist in the pull between two people. It couldn't just be her...

"We're absolutely not attracted to each other at all, right...?"

"It's fine," he said again, giving his arm another dismissive glance. He turned away, scrubbed a hand over the back of his neck, picked up his bottle of water.

"Right," she said. "Good."

"Are you tired? Should we...erm..." He gestured to the bed.

"Yeah..." And then, forcing her voice into brisk breeziness, "Yes! Let's One-Bed, roomie."

He chuckled. She laughed. They got into the bed, each on their own side.

It would be fine. They weren't attracted to each other. They had Various Good Reasons.

They would lie there all night, close together, not touching. And totally not desperate for each other

He chuckled again, wriggling into position. She laughed.

Hah-hah-hah... Keep laughing, pretend she wasn't nearly hyperventilating...

"I think we're meant to build a wall of pillows between us," she said. "Or insist on sleeping head to toe."

And you should definitely have more clothes on.

"Or..." he suggested off-handedly, folding an arm behind his head on his pillow and flashing her a grin. "We could just sleep together in this bed like normal grown adults and absolutely not have sex?"

"Yeah," she muttered. "That too."

She lay down. She pulled up her side of the duvet. His was only at his waist. She could see the skin of his shoulder out of the corner of the eye. Will turned off his bedside light. She turned off hers. She could *still* see the skin of his shoulder, gleaming in the faint moonlight.

"So. Here we are," he said. "Two grown adults. Alone in bed together. Completely unattracted to each other. It's nice, isn't it? Relaxing."

"Yeah. So relaxing."

She lay entirely rigid, staring straight up into blackness.

"Such a good idea to share this room."

"Shut up, Will."

"I'm really looking forward to all this sleep we're going to have."

"You're meant to sleep on the floor."
"You sleep on the floor."
"No."
"Fine. Let's go to sleep then."
"Yep. Sleep. Good idea."
"Night, Jules."
"Night, Will."
Silence.
Silence.
Torture.

William shifted slightly. The movement tugged on the duvet, scraping it over her body. Over her breasts, her tingling nipples. She was burning. Heart pounding. Core throbbing.

One Bed was *hell*.

"Jules," Will said, his voice hushed in the dark.

"Yes?"

"Is it still the one bed trope if the people just give in and have sex?"

Chapter 12

Not unsurprisingly, Jules took a moment to answer.

He probably should not have said that. No. He *definitely* should not have said that. Now it was hanging in the dark between them, stretched out on the silence, buffeted by the exhale of Jules' breath.

"I think that might be...um...considered a subversion of the trope," she answered, very carefully, as though she were picking her way through a minefield.

Will nodded, which was stupid, given it was dark and she couldn't see. But he was feeling incredibly stupid right now.

Hence asking that question. And then saying:

"So if the guy said to the girl something like, 'I'm insanely attracted to you. And not touching you is killing me.' That would be subverting the trope too?"

He heard her swallow. She was so close beside him he could hear her every breath. "Why...um... Why do you ask?" she said.

"Literary curiosity."

"Right."

His heart was pounding, his muscles wound so tight it almost hurt. The woman beside him was blazing like a beacon. And she was Jay's *sister*, who hated men, who thought he was a clown—and a few minutes ago he had come so close to kissing her that the wrench of stepping back might be a scar branded on his soul forever.

He'd come out of the bathroom and she had been in her pyjamas, totally mismatched things. Soft cotton trousers, cosy waffle fabric, well-washed and worn. And a silk top, edged in lace. All of it black, of course. That was the only thing that matched.

He'd never had a relationship long enough to reach that imperfect stage of tatty pyjamas, mismatched underwear, odd socks with holes in. Never quite reached the unvarnished truth of a person. But there Jules was, perfectly imperfect, makeup-free and hair down and vulnerable and raw and there—there, at his side, concern in her voice and eyes as she touched his bruise.

God. All of that had been as intoxicating as anything else. As the look of her breasts in the black silk top, braless, the peaks of her nipples clear through the thin fabric. He could imagine how they'd feel, the heavy swell of flesh in his hand, the warm silk sliding...

He wanted her so badly. But he couldn't, they couldn't—

"They're not meant to admit it," Jules said, her quiet voice setting his heart thundering. "The attraction. They fight it all night long."

"Do they sleep?"

"No. They spend a terrible night."

"Sounds like torture."

"Yeah. It is."

A beat of deep silence.

Will said, "So the man doesn't tell her that he thinks she's beautiful?"

A whisper. "No."

"That he really, really likes her?"

"No."

"That he's aching to touch her? That he's been fighting it all day? That he's jealous of his own car's seatbelt because it's been slotted between her breasts for hours and that's exactly where he'd like to be?"

"That's...highly specific."

His laugh was a breath in the dark. "I can't think where the inspiration came from. But does he ever say that? The man in bed with the woman he can't touch?"

"No. And...and the woman doesn't tell him how much she craves that touch. That she's aching too. That she's...she's wet just thinking about it."

"Fuck."

If he'd thought he was horny before, it was nothing to the madness of the craving her admission ignited.

"Jules..."

"Yes?"

He swallowed, throat dry. "It's interesting, this idea of subverting the trope. Don't you think?"

There was a smile in her voice. "Are you trying to use literary analysis to get into my pants?"

"I'm suspecting it's the only thing that might work."

She laughed lightly. He felt the tremor of it through the

mattress.

"Not the only thing," she admitted, a weight of meaning behind the quiet confession.

"Oh?"

"Just you being you, Will. The real you. That's enough."

That floored him. Set off a piercing wave in his chest that left him dizzy. He couldn't think, couldn't find words; his body was on fire, already hers, and now his mind... His mind was reeling as though reality itself had tilted.

She was waiting for him to say something. He knew that. Her words demanded an answer. All he could do was reach out through the dark, under the covers, and find her hand.

Their fingers twined together. He felt her turn towards him. "Shall we?" she said. "Have sex? Subvert this trope? Make it our bitch?"

He breathed a laugh. "I would love to."

"OK... So... Will? You're just holding my hand."

He nodded. "I know. It's just... That already feels like a lot, doesn't it?"

"It does," she agreed quietly.

He lay there a moment longer, trying to gather his wits, embarrassingly aware that he was being too soft, too mushy, too pathetic. Where was his game? What would his friends think of him? A gorgeous girl literally asking him to have sex with her and him lying there holding her hand, stupidly close to tears?

Fuck. He let out a breath. He turned his head towards her. He could make out the glint of her eyes in the dark. Playful, inviting... And he felt like a schoolboy, as though he'd never kissed anyone, the dizzying anticipation of it twisting his gut with tight, sharp desire.

He moved closer, tracing the curve of her cheek with his free hand. Her breath hitched, her exhale caught somewhere there behind her lips. So he bent his head, brushed his mouth over hers to find it. She released it with a murmur, the faintest groan as he kissed her fully, her lips soft and giving against his.

The world stilled. There was only her. There was nothing but her and the sounds she made and the feel of her mouth moving with his.

"Jules..." he breathed, as though he was lost and asking her to find him in the dark.

And she did, her mouth opening to his, inviting him into the warmth, bringing him deeper with every slide and gasp and touch of her tongue. Her hands cupped his face, pushed into his hair, held firm to the nape of his neck and brought his mouth down harder until their kiss was a filthy, desperate thing. A kiss that drove hands searching, feverishly exploring.

He moved over her, thigh slipping between her legs as she ground against him. His hand spanned the edge of her ribs, slipped up under her top to the silk and velvet of her breast. He groaned against her mouth, breathing hard.

"I want to see you," he said. "I need to see you."

"OK."

A breathless exchange, him reaching for the bedside table, clumsily searching for the light. He flicked it on, and there she was. Jules. Lips red and silver eyes glazed. A dream woman made real.

She sat up a little and pulled off her top.

"I fucking love this trope," he growled, and his mouth found hers again.

Kissing William wasn't anything like she had imagined. It was terrifying. Because every press of his mouth unstitched her soul. He was tearing her down the seam, opening her heart. And she couldn't let him have it.

This wasn't about that. This was just sex. The fun part, as he had teased her earlier. So long ago.

She'd given in to the temptation of him, deciding it was just another thing to be experienced, like saying yes to this room when life threw it in her path.

One Bed, why not? It'd be funny, right?

William Shilstone, why not? He was nice and attractive, and she wanted him. No harm in that. Or so she had reasoned, lying there with her pulse racing, skin burning, hearing him admit he wanted her too.

But she hadn't expected him to hold her hand. She hadn't expected his kisses to bring hidden, forced-back tears. How could she? No one had ever kissed her like he did. As though he wanted every part of her, body and soul. And she hadn't bargained on his touch being like worship. The blazing Old Testament kind. All fire and eternal sin.

He looked down at her when the light came on, pupils wide and drugged and dirty, his gaze stroking over her bare breasts, before he pinned her to the bed with another life-altering kiss.

"This is OK?" he breathed, mouth skating over her throat. "You still want this?"

"Yes. Yes..." Then she couldn't do anything but moan as his mouth captured her nipple, his tongue sending swirls of pleasure to gather at the ache in her core.

It would be OK... She would survive this. Him. He moved to her other breast, her fingers wrapping into his hair, and she no longer cared about the wreck he was making of her heart. It felt too good. Was worth the pain.

He moved down her body, kissing a line from her ribs. Her hands slid from his hair as he curled his fingers into the waistband of her pyjamas, pulling them down along with her knickers.

She was bare to him. Naked and heated and wanting. His dark gaze knew it, mirrored her need. He looked down her body, greedily taking it in as he spread her legs and kneeled, hand already stroking up the inside of her thigh.

"This trope..." he murmured. "Do they ever say 'I'm going to fuck you with my tongue?'"

"No." She gasped as his hand reached her slick core, fingers trailing almost idly over her entrance as he smiled—a new type of smile. A little wicked. "That might..." she said, biting back a moan, "ruin the pretence of them not liking each other."

"Like this does?" he asked, rubbing a fingertip along her opening. "Him touching her and finding her dripping wet? That might give the game away."

"Maybe. A little."

He pushed a finger inside, eyes devouring the way she bit her lip.

"A smidgen?" he asked. "Is that how hot she finds him?"
"Yes."
"Yes?"
"Yes..." She no longer knew what they were saying, had lost her train of thought. He was working her with one finger, thumb brushing her clit. He leant down, bracing an arm by her side as his mouth captured her nipple, grazing the tender tip with his tongue before he sucked, just as the finger inside crooked, brushing that spot that made her see stars.

She bucked her hips, tried to squirm away, fighting the climax that was building. *Too soon, too soon.* She wanted this to last.

"You promised me tongue," she gasped.

He chuckled and licked her nipple. "Like this?"

"You know what I mean."

"Say it. Please."

He met her eyes, still holding himself braced over her on one hand, his other now spanning her hip. He was asking, not commanding, the heat in his eyes a delicious contrast to the boyish flush on his cheeks.

"I want you..." she began.

"Yes?" He touched her again, as though unable to stop himself.

"I want you to..." She broke off with a moan as he slid two fingers inside her, slowly, exploring, testing... "Fuck..."

He watched his fingers move in and out. "Fuck?"

"Yes..."

"With?"

"Anything... Everything..."

She barely heard what response he made. He kept his fingers working her slowly as he settled between her legs. Just the touch of his hair against her thigh was almost too much. Then his mouth was there, his breath hot sin against her wet flesh. He added tongue to the torturous slide of his fingers, caressing the slick folds and edges, adding pleasure to pleasure, then bringing his mouth to her clit and sucking, so that she swore, twisting away from him, seconds from coming. *Not yet, not yet.*

She felt the breath of his soft laugh. He knew, damn him. He knew how close she was, and he was playing with her, teasing her, threatening to tip her over the edge again and again until she was mindless, caught on an endless wave of that spiralling moment just before, when everything was too much but not quite enough...

"Will, Will..."

He moved, she heard a rustle of foil and opened drugged eyes to see him getting a condom from his wallet on the bedside table. "OK?" he asked her, before he ripped it open.

She nodded and watched him roll it on. He was hard and smooth, his body so tense that she knew the way he had been torturing her had been almost as unbearable for him. The realisation of how badly he wanted this shot a new wave of anticipation through her.

He moved over her, resting his weight on one forearm, his other hand cupping her face, bringing her eyes to his, forcing her to give up another piece of her fraying, shattered heart.

This meant something. That's what his look said. Not

a notch on his bedpost, not a meaningless thing to be forgotten in a day or a week.

Something that would put a stitch in both their souls.

He kissed her. So gently it brought more tears. But he didn't see, because she closed her eyes, and his head was bent, his mouth against her ear, whispering, "I like you so much, Jules. I like you so fucking much."

He moved inside her, so easily it felt like coming home. He fitted her perfectly, the stretch and the slide of him, the angle just right.

"I like you too," she whispered, clutching him to her as he rocked into her and she fell apart.

Chapter 13

Jules' head was on his chest, her dark hair tickling his rib cage with every breath. Divine torment. Which about summed up Jules Orton.

No... Right now...? Just divine.

He didn't have it in him to feel ticklish anyway. He was too comfortable, too relaxed, deep contentment in every...erm...bone of his body.

If he'd been worried he might cry *before* sleeping with Jules, he now had to acknowledge he was a broken man. Nothing, and no one, had ever felt so good.

"I like this Christmas present I've unwrapped," he murmured. His arm was around her, his hand stroking up and down her back, her side, the rollercoaster dip of her waist. "It's the best one I've ever had." Her arm was draped across his stomach, tracing circles on his bare hip.

Divine torment.

He heard the smile in her voice as she said, "Mine looked like it had been wrapped by a clown, but it turned out alright, once I got past that."

He huffed a laugh, lightly pinching the skin of her hip.

Drowsy silence reigned, then she asked, "Why does

everyone call you Biffy?" Her voice was sleepy, muffled against his skin.

"It's from my great granddad. I was named after him."

"So that's why you're William Shilstone the Second. I always wondered." He felt her cheek curve against his chest, the feel of a smile forming. "William *Augustus Henry* Shilstone the Second, sorry."

"I know. Hard to believe they saddled two people with that."

"And Biffy was his nickname?"

"Yes. From when he was in the RAF, I think. I always assumed it was some variation of Billy. But no one knows for sure."

"He was a pilot?"

"Second World War. Got shot down over the Channel during the Battle of Britain. Never recovered the body or the plane."

She lifted her head, sympathy in her eyes.

"A very long time ago, Jules."

He stroked his favourite path down her side again, until she settled her head back against his chest. "So it's a hero's name. I should have known."

His hand slowed as he tried to make sense of that. She hadn't sounded teasing. She sounded…sad.

"Are you OK?"

"Yes, yes. Just tired. What time is it?"

He reached for his phone, trying not to disturb the way she lay against him. "Just gone two."

"We should sleep. It's still a long drive to Fel's tomorrow."

Right. Fel. Yes.

Will stared up at the ceiling, a silence settling between them as he tried to think of a way to explain... *Jules, you know your best friend who I've been obsessed with for years and who, only this morning, I openly declared I'd drive eight hundred miles for? Well... The thing is... I've been labouring under a misapprehension.*

Wasn't that a *Pride and Prejudice* quote? At least Jules might appreciate that.

"I texted her," Jules said. "When I let her know to expect me tomorrow. I told her you were with me. I asked if we could stay for lunch. See. I'm the very finest in charity wingmen."

Will froze, hand stopping. "Jules..."

She sat up and stretched, her back to him. He watched the soft skin shift over the small bones of her spine, her ribs, a presentiment of doom closing his throat. She began to hunt for her discarded pyjamas, heedless of her nakedness. Of his.

"Jules. I think we need to talk—"

"I'll give you some hot topics of conversation on the drive down," she said over him, finding her top under a scattered pillow. "Things you can say in case you get tongue-tied. Basically, Will, it's horses." She winked as she tugged her pyjama trousers up before heading to the bathroom. "Pretend you love horses and you'll be golden."

The bathroom door closed. Will sat up in bed, queasy, heart beating shakily as he stared at the closed door.

Had he just been One-Night-Standed by an Orton? Him and a fifth of the country.

"I said I don't date, Will. Not that I don't have sex."

That's what she'd said when he'd teased her about her love life. *I don't date.*

Love is a myth.

You are a clown.

At what point had he forgotten all of the warnings she'd freely given him? At what point on their journey had he succumbed to the chemical brain-goo she so derided and appeared immune to?

Was it when she held his hand and squeezed it back?

Was it when she clung to him and moaned his name?

Was it when she whispered, *"I like you, I like you too..."*

Liked him to fuck? Liked him to fool around and subvert a *book trope* with? That should have been a clue, shouldn't it? This was all some weird wish-fulfilment game. A literary bucket-list item to tick off.

Fuck. He really had been One-Night-Standed by an Orton. No wonder Jay got so many dark looks.

It was devastating.

Jules didn't wake tangled in Will's arms, or spooning him, or with his hand possessively across her stomach. Or even with him staring creepily at her while she slept.

Because this was real life, not fiction. So she woke alone on her side of the bed, William's back to her. He was so far on his side it was a wonder he hadn't fallen off in his sleep.

If he even was asleep. It was hard to tell. But his shoulders looked tense, the sweeps of muscle held firm. She fought an urge to slide her hand up between his shoulder blades, press it into the curve where neck met shoulder, soothe and knead and stroke until those shoulders relaxed, and he turned to look at her, smiling...

Smiling because he was only hours from seeing Fel?

Smiling because of what they had done last night?

Or, worse than any of those, smiling because he thought she would smile back and crawl into the arms he held out to her. But she couldn't. She *couldn't*.

She sat up and thought he flinched. But when she passed him on the way to the bathroom, his eyes were firmly shut.

She brushed her teeth, eyeing her reflection critically, thinking it ought to look changed, dark and dissipated, Dorian Gray's portrait. She hated the morning after. Her usual tactic was to leave, preferably straightaway. At least before the other person woke.

Instead, they would spend hours together in a car.

She hoped he wasn't going to be weird about it. Surely he'd done this far more often than she had. She spat her foaming toothpaste into the sink and wondered what sort of notch his friend's sister would make in his bedpost. A deeper one than usual? Or a guilty scratch?

"I like you so much."

His voice, the feel of those words, the feel of him all around her, inside her. The memory clouded her thoughts, stole reality for a moment and replaced it with a dream.

But no. *No.* She shook her head. She'd decided what last night would be before he ever took hold of her hand. The only thing it could be. Nothing but sex. Good sex. *Fright-*

eningly good sex. It couldn't be anything else, not with a man who would sleep with her while openly declaring he was halfway in love with someone else.

"It's not like you've been saving yourself for your one true love."

"This isn't some medieval fairy story. I'm not insane."

Was *she*? Was she insane to think there might be a man out there who would want *her* and only her and never stray? A man like the heroes in the stories, who fell so hard for just one girl they never looked at another?

Maybe that *was* mad. Maybe people would always look. Everyone was human. Everyone had eyes. But their heart... Their heart... Couldn't that at least stay true?

All she knew was that she couldn't end up like her mother. Jessica and Jay believed she put up with her husband's infidelities because she cared only for his title, his money, his house. But Jules knew better. She could tell from the bitterness of her mother's tears, the strength of her anger when the two of them shook the house with screams... She loved him. You had to care for it to hurt that much.

The simplest way to protect oneself was not to care.

Especially from a man like William. Because he was dangerously close to stealing her heart. And she knew that if she let him, she would never get it back again. Even when he grew bored of it and tossed it aside, it would still be his. Because Jules knew that if she fell, she would fall forever.

Chapter 14

WHEN JULES CAME OUT of the bathroom, she found William up, standing by the tea and coffee machine on the sideboard. He passed her a cup with a smile.

It was a perfect smile. Perfectly formed. Perfectly bland and featureless. She took the cup, realising his imperturbable good nature might be as much a shield against the world as her cynical disdain.

"Christmas Eve," he commented, walking to his bag to pick out some clothes and things for the shower. "Doesn't much feel like it in here, I suppose."

He went into the bathroom, leaving her to ponder if there was a rebuke hidden in his mild tone. Though he was right. It was still dark outside, the winter sun not yet up. The light from the bulbs seemed watery, leaving the edges of the room brown, the shadows like damp leaves piled in the corners. No cheer. No comfort. Just two half-empty bags and a pretty but soulless room wishing them gone.

Downstairs, the foyer was little better. It was early, hardly anyone about. The air smelt of the cleaner's round just finished, detergent and stale mop; and the Christmas lights decorating the foyer's tree and the edges of the desk were unlit.

They checked out and climbed into the cold car. The sat nav still held Fel's address.

Four hours, fifty-seven minutes.
Estimated time of arrival: 13:12.

"I hope the traffic's better," said Jules as they pulled out of the hotel car park.

"Yeah."

"At least it didn't snow in the night."

"Yeah."

"How are your bruises today?"

"Fine."

"Is everything OK?"

He glanced at her, eyebrow raised. "We're just forgetting the whole sleeping together thing, are we? Pretending it didn't happen?"

"No, let's make it really awkward instead."

He let out a sharp sigh. Exasperation. Anger.

"What, Will? Am I meant to buy you flowers? A ring? We're on our way to see *Fel*, remember? The girl you're crazy for?"

"I'm not—" He stopped.

"Not what?"

He smashed the stick clumsily down the gears as they slowed for a T-junction. "I told you. I'm not in love with her."

"It's been her for eight years, Will."

"But—"

"But what? You've got some post-coital glow thing going on and you're confusing it for something else?"

"For fuck's sake, Jules."

"Right. Yeah. Articulate."

She sat back angrily in the seat, arms folded, flushed with guilt as much as anything else. She wasn't being nice. And William didn't deserve that. But he also didn't deserve her heart. That's what it felt like he was asking for: her to admit it had meant something; her to admit how much she liked him; her to admit she knew he wasn't really in love with Fel—had known it even before he did.

To admit she had always, in some small way, known him better than he knew himself.

But that was too big. That all meant too much. Her stomach twisted at the thought of it, and she forced herself not to feel it, to cross her arms and stare out of the window and stoke her anger instead.

"It was just sex, Will. Don't turn it into more than it was."

Driving kept Will sane. *Think about the road, the traffic, overtake that car, change lane, change gear.* That part of his mind was smooth and detached and in control.

The other was reeling. He didn't know what was going on. Was he suddenly in love with Jules? Overnight? Just like that? No wonder she didn't believe him.

Or maybe this was just the beginning of love. The start of falling. A disorienting panorama suddenly yawning wide open beneath him, like pulling back the door on a plane before a parachute jump, being buffeted by forces bigger than you, barely knowing which way was up.

So many ways for things to go wrong.

To get hurt.

Jules sat silent and stiff beside him for mile after mile. It had been an hour since they last spoke. Since their argument, if such a mess of half-said things even deserved that name.

"It was just sex, Will. Don't turn it into more than it was."

He had nodded, angry, the jerk of his head the only reply he could muster. And nothing more had been said.

What else was there to say?

He was the man who had switched allegiance from his unrequited crush to her best friend the moment they hopped into bed together. He knew how that must look. It was shitty, and he had no defence other than that it had seemed right at the time. Inevitable. As necessary as breathing.

Fucking blissful.

But in the cold light of day...

"We're on our way to see Fel, remember? The girl you're crazy for?"

He winced. Visibly so. Jules' head turned towards him, then just as swiftly turned back.

Oh, the *irony* of spending years aping the worst behaviours of the worst players, and then, at the very moment it mattered, being caught in the splashback. Jules saw him as a slut. Expected nothing else. Wasn't even *surprised*.

Because she hadn't protested, had she, last night? Didn't

put a hand to his chest and say, *"Wait, what about Fel?"* She knew Fel meant nothing to him. Knew all his pretensions to a grand romance were hollow. And she had no reason to worry it would hurt Fel. They both knew Fel barely even knew he existed.

No. Jules had known exactly what last night was. *"The fun stuff,"* he'd jokingly called it. *"The physical act of love..."*

Not love. Just sex. Nothing else. Not to Jules, who believed love was a myth and all its attendant emotions nothing but chemical goo.

Why would she believe it had been real for him? The man whose only notions of love and romance were laughably teenagerish? Who thought he was in love when he wasn't? Who slept with a girl when he shouldn't?

A man who clearly had no idea what he was fucking doing. Who appeared to think only with his dick, just like every other loser she so rightly detested.

How on earth did he prove otherwise?

His phone rang, connecting automatically to the hands-free. He grimaced at the name on the screen. Vikram Singh.

"Hi, Vik."

"Biffy! You disappeared from Deveron before we got a chance to discuss New Year."

"Yeah. Had a long drive."

"What's the plan, man? Nothing's sorted. No one knows where to be. Tristan Shady keeps bolloxing on about Vegas. I heard someone say Bali? Hugo doesn't give a shit. Tell us you've got something planned? I don't even care if it's at Hurl Up Cote, so long as you can get rid of your old folks."

Will flashed Jules an apologetic look. Her face was impassive.

"I don't know, Vik. I've not planned anything."

"The fuck you say? Come on, man. We're relying on you. Gang's falling apart. Look the fuck at Jay. What the fuck's that all about? You need to plan something epic, Biff. Tempt him back on the game."

"You plan it, Vik."

"Fuck off, Biffy. I'm not planning shit. That's your job."

Will tensed, palms sweating, very much wishing Jules was not hearing any of this. Then, laughing, Vik said, "Oh, fuck, Biff, I just remembered! Someone said you got stuck giving Jay's psycho little sister a ride home yesterday? Fucking hell. It's not even like you can tap that to make up for the torture. Though you always did like the weird ones. Look at The Fell Pennington. Pity she only fucks hor—"

He reached for the dash and cut the call.

"Well," said Jules. "That was edifying. Impressive use of the F-bomb. Almost a sort of..." She waved her hand. "Modern poetry?"

"My friends are dicks." It was as much confession as apology.

"I know. I grew up with one." She paused. "What I can't understand is why you hang around with them by *choice*."

He grimaced. "They're not all bad. You must know that. Jay's a good guy. Even Hugo. It's mostly hot air."

"Boys being boys?" she asked sardonically.

He almost tried to explain. Tried to voice how, in the awful soul-jarring intensity of being at boarding school, surrounded by nothing but equally lost boys, all of you cast into that same sea of testosterone and hidden homesickness, one learnt to sink or swim. Friendships were a lifeline, and you learnt to hold on at all costs, no matter how nauseating the ride.

But even if things had been fine between him and Jules, he might have hesitated. She would think he was excusing the inexcusable. Though there was a vast world of nuance between a reason and an excuse. *Boys will be boys...* Yes, because sometimes boys didn't have much choice. Not when they were only human, their character barely formed...

But Jules had been to boarding school too. That's where she'd met Fel. So maybe it *was* just an excuse. He frowned at the road ahead.

"They use you," she said quietly.

"Yes," he admitted. "But they're still my friends. People are always using someone for something. Even if they don't realise it. Even if they don't mean to."

She didn't answer. She might think he was having a dig at her. Saying that, last night, she had used him. That's certainly how it felt to him now, but it wasn't at all what he meant. And it was only wounded pride. Unrequited...feelings. He had been the one to initiate things. It wasn't Jules' fault that he had suddenly decided he wanted more. That he had suddenly realised he *felt* more. That he had been blind...

"People are all incomplete," he tried to explain. "We all...have gaps. Parts of us that need something you can only get from other people."

He felt her eyes on him, imagined the sceptical frown.

He almost wished she would make some cutting remark, attack him with sarcasm. It would have been better than this cool silence.

"I'm a nerd, Jules. And soft. I've been spoilt my whole life. I needed the cool boys... I needed..." He waved a hand in a gesture that immediately reminded him of her. "I've always had anything I've ever wanted, but that doesn't help a person understand who they are. I needed to experience other things, darker things. Find the edges of myself. The lines I wouldn't cross."

"You could have found better role models, Will."

"Maybe I didn't want to." His sudden irritation took him by surprise. But he was tired of explaining himself to someone who would never care. Why was she even bothering to ask? "Maybe it's fun, the life they lead."

"Exactly. They lead. And you follow."

"They're my friends," he repeated, the words curt. Final. Because maybe they did use him, but at least they didn't loathe him. They didn't tempt him to bare his soul, then pick it apart and sneer at what they found.

They didn't outright reject him.

"You can do better."

Except her voice wasn't sneering. It was gentle. And that was far worse.

It felt like pity.

"If you want to find out who you really are... I think you'd do better looking inside. That's...that's where the good stuff is."

She said the last part very quietly, then trailed off into silence. A heavy, choking silence like smog that burnt eyes and throat. The kind you couldn't see a way through.

Will drove.

The motorway ground on, little sign of Christmas anywhere, except in the lighted windows of the lorry drivers, or the occasional car boot piled high with presents. The fields were chilled and grey, the sky heavy, never properly getting light even as the day drew toward noon.

They reached the M25. Started to circle London. Signs for Kent appeared. Maidstone, Ashford, Canterbury.

One hour to go.

"Everyone's there," Jules said suddenly, her casual conversational tone jarring after the long silence. "Fel said. Everyone except Ethan. He's still off travelling somewhere. Totally AWOL. It's driving everyone nuts now he's the new Viscount. Apparently they need him to sign some legal documents and things."

"Right," said Will, so far from caring about the Penningtons he could weep.

"Even Charles is there. He's on leave. Hasn't been back in months. I can barely remember when I last saw him."

Will grunted. Charles Pennington, RAF Officer. Tall and strapping and dark and handsome, well over six foot, just like all the Pennington men, even James, who was barely out of his teens. No doubt Charles looked bloody wonderful in his uniform. He could regale Jules with tales of heroism and derring-do, and look exactly like one of the soldier-princes in her books while he did it.

His grip tightened on the steering wheel.

"Cate's there, Cessy too. And Cessy is in charge of the cooking, so there'll definitely be enough food for you at lunch. Do you know they call her Excessy, because she does everything to excess?"

Will flashed Jules a glance. Was she trying to torture him by prattling on about the Penningtons? Because this gossipy, non-stop chat wasn't her usual style.

Or maybe she was holding out what she saw as an olive branch. Offering him this conversational topic as a way of pretending that everything was exactly how it had been twenty-four hours ago. It was the Penningtons he was driving to see. It was Felicity on his mind. Nothing had changed, everything was fine between them.

They could still be friends.

Was that what he wanted? To pretend last night had meant nothing and carry on just being Jules' sort-of-friend? Her brother's annoying friend who hung around a lot, hoping for a sight of Fel, completely oblivious to the girl right under his nose?

No. He didn't want that at all. And besides, it was impossible. He couldn't go back to seeing Jules as anything other than what she was.

Beautiful. Devastating.

But maybe sort-of-friends was all she could give him. Because he suddenly realised—suddenly understood—that if he kept pressing her about last night, kept trying to pursue this thing between them, she would retreat. Push back. Disappear completely from his life. And the thought of that was bleak.

"Well." He forced a smile. "Not long to go now."

Chapter 15

There had been Penningtons in Kent for over four hundred years, and the central part of Fraversham Hall—the knapped flint wall of the entrance porch—was almost that old.

But Jules and Will went round the side to the kitchen, just like everyone always did.

They walked from the car in silence except for the crunch of their feet on the thin gravel. It was worn to nothing in places, showing the bare chalky soil, pale and compacted almost as hard as stone. In other places, it was puddled with rainwater, black mirrors reflecting the dark clouds.

If William Shilstone was the richest of her friends, the Penningtons were the poorest.

The Hall was a long rectangular building, only two stories high. The gravel drive surrounded it on three sides, the bases of the house's walls all hemmed with half-wild plants and bushes and climbing roses. At the back of the house was the lawn and gardens, just as overgrown. Jules loved it.

It was bitter now though, the threat of sleet heavy in the

iron sky, and she longed to be inside. Will was silent and stiff beside her as they approached the kitchen door. There was a warm glow of light coming through the small panes of glass and the narrow window at the door's side. She could imagine the chaos of voices within. Six Penningtons. Five siblings and their mother. She quailed a little at the thought even as she hurried to meet it.

Mostly, it would be a relief to hand William off. Present him to Fel, mission accomplished. Let other people dilute the awful tension between them. Let her forget it. Pretend it wasn't her fault. Ignore the churning guilt that kept prompting her to fix it, to bring the sunshine back to William's smile. But how? How? She couldn't give him what he wanted.

He didn't even know what he wanted. More sex? A few dates? A week or a month to try her out and see if they worked? If commitment was something he could commit to?

They stopped at the door. Jules' heart thumped. Will looked at her, so many things in his expression, she couldn't untangle them all, only knew it would hurt to try, like plunging her hand into the wild rose that grew unplanned by the door.

"Finally," she said, forcing a smile, wondering just when she had become the one who smiled so falsely, and Will the one who looked so sour. "Here we are."

"Here we are," he echoed.

"Ready?"

"No."

But she drowned his bitter reply with the force of her

knock. *Thump, thump, thump,* on the ancient wood. Who would answer the door? Exuberant Cessy? Dutiful Cate? Gracious Charles?

No. It was Fel.

Jules stared stupidly for a moment, feeling almost like Will must, that Fel was a mythical creature, not a real blood-and-flesh girl. Her friend had taken on such epic proportions in her mind over the last two days, had been the revolving point of so many of her thoughts, so many of her and Will's conversations, that, for a moment, she was struck dumb.

Fel spoke first, smiling her shy smile as she tucked glossy hair behind her ear. "Jules. You made it." She flashed Will an uncertain glance. "And you're...um...Billy, right? Jules said you're coming for lunch?"

Jules felt him flinch at the misnaming. She felt it too, a blow as though to her own heart. *Eight years, eight hundred miles, and she doesn't know his name...*

Will took a step back, shaking his head. "No, thank you. But I... My parents are waiting for me. I need to get going." He turned, giving them both a tight, undirected smile, eyes elsewhere. And walked away. Back to his car.

Fel opened the door wider. "Come in. It's so cold—"

But Jules hardly heard the words, or the voices of Cessy and Charles from somewhere inside, laughingly singing a line or two.

Last Christmas, I gave you my heart...

"Hang on. I left something in the car."

She hurried after Will.

The car was parked at the edge of the gravelled forecourt,

near a long and towering hedge of yew. Will's hand was on the driver's door, shoulders hunched against the cold.

"Wait! Will... I'm so sorry..."

He turned and regarded her for a moment or two, scanning her breathless, shivering self with a smile that held only ice.

"You're sorry? Why? Because she didn't know my name? No one does, do they? *I* don't even know my own name. Biffy? Will? Who the fuck cares."

"I care. I—"

"Yeah. Right—you said you saw the real me, the person I was inside. Do you remember that? I sure as hell can't forget it. But did you even mean it? Or was it just some crap you learnt off Jay to get someone into bed with you?"

She recoiled. "What? No!" He was accusing *her* of being the one to hit and run? With *his* reputation? "It's not like you needed much persuading, Will. Even for a guy supposedly in love with someone else."

He flushed, but his eyes glittered with anger.

"So you hate me because I slept with you? Would I have had a better chance if I'd pretended to care for Fel, faked some devotion I didn't feel? I told you I didn't love her—"

"I don't hate you—"

"I told you I didn't, but you knew that already. I made a mistake. I was barely nineteen the first time I saw her. I was a kid with a crush and I never grew up enough to realise that's all it was until—"

He broke off, scrubbed a hand through his hair. It was sleeting, Jules realised. Freezing and wet and sharp, falling on her cheeks, in her eyes.

"Until?" she asked, not heeding the cold.

"Until I felt something real." His face softened, eyes searching hers as he took a step towards her. "I know it's shitty timing. I know how it must look, that it's far from ideal, but I think this is real, isn't it? I feel—"

"No." She shook her head, thoughts ringing. "Don't."

"What?"

"Don't ask me for this, I don't—I can't—" She didn't know what she was saying, was scrabbling for words, flinging them up like a barricade. "I don't date, Will. I told you. I *told* you."

"You *told* me that you liked me. You told me I was *nice*. You told me a lot of things, Jules. Not just with your words, but with how it felt, last night. That didn't all come from me. That...that *connection*, it needs two people—"

"You're some expert now? After years of thinking you felt something you didn't, I'm meant to believe you're suddenly sure what you're feeling?"

"No. But I think it's worth finding out. Don't you?"

She shook her head, quickly, desperately, denying the whole situation not just his words. But his jaw clenched, muscle ticking. "You won't even give me a chance?"

"I can't..."

"Because I'm not worth it? Because you don't like me enough? Is it the thunderbolt you're waiting for? That love-at-first-sight world-stopping bollocks I preached in the car? Because it's not all it's cracked up to be, believe me. Maybe it doesn't happen like that. Not for everyone. Maybe sometimes it takes time and getting to know someone, and it creeps up on you so gradually, you're falling in love before you even realise what's happening—"

"It's because I'm scared."

Her voice was small, but it silenced him instantly. He made to move towards her, eyes shadowed with searching concern. She held up her hand, keeping him back.

"I'm scared. Because if I let this mean something, it will mean *everything*. And I can't... I refuse... I can't end up like my mother, in love with a man who doesn't love her back, who spent his youth sleeping with everything that moved and never stopped, even once he was married—"

"You think I'm like your *father?*" Will's voice broke in horror on the word. "You think I'd do the things he does? Treat you the way he treats your mother?"

"No, but—"

"What was all the stuff you said about me being nice? About liking me for *me*? Why would you say that?"

"I do like you."

"Your father's a bully. And a coward. And a lech. And you think that's *me?*"

"No... But... How can I ever be sure?"

"By trusting me, Jules! By knowing me."

"How can I? You don't... You barely even know yourself."

His face clouded. He was hurt, and it hurt her. She wanted so badly to go to him, soothe him, cup his face in her hands and clear the shadow from his eyes. But...

"I want to *know*, Will. I want to know with every fibre of my being that the man I'm with will never lie and go behind my back, or break my heart, or get bored with me and start getting his kicks elsewhere. I need to *know*. But I can't. Not if he...if he doesn't even know his own mind."

He didn't speak for a moment. A lesser man might have ranted and raved and stormed away. But he absorbed what she said in grim silence, eyes on hers. Eventually, he nodded.

"You want complete certainty? You want everlasting love and nothing else?"

She didn't speak. What could she say? That, yes, she was holding out for a fairytale? For the impossible?

"It's always going to be a risk, Jules. Falling in love. It's a risk I'm prepared to take."

He held her eyes for a moment more, sleet frosting his hair, his shoulders, wet on his cheeks. She said nothing, as though the ice falling all around them had crept inside, frozen her from the inside out.

He waited, giving her one last chance. Then he opened his car door, pausing long enough to say:

"Jules... The only way to guarantee you won't find love is to never risk trying."

Chapter 16

25th December

Will:
Merry Christmas

Jules:
Merry Christmas, Will

31st December

Jules:
Happy New Year, Will x

Will:
Happy New Year x

14th February

Will:
<message deleted>
Sry. Drunk.
Txted wrong number

Jules:
That's OK.
How are you?

Will:
Fine
Drunk
But fine
You weren't at L+P's engagement party?

Jules:
No
I was in Paris
And he's only a distant cousin

Will:
We're going to be cousins-in-law
If that's a thing?
How was Paris?

Jules:
Terrible

The guy I was with kept calling it the City of Love
And saying English words in a French accent
Like that was the same as speaking French?

Will:
Push him in the Seine

Jules:
Hah. It was tempting.

Will:
I'll do it for you

Jules:
Can't ask you to kill for me

Will:
I mean a dunking, you assume murder
This is how we differ

Jules:
:p
You would have wanted to kill him
But he's my boss
Might not pass my probation if I kill/dunk him

Will:
Boss?
It was a work trip?

Jules:
Yeah

Will:
Right. That's cool
I mean, that you get to travel for work
New job?
Publishing?

Jules:
Yeah

Will:
Sorry. Gtg. Being thrown out of bar.
Vik's fault
Possibly Hugo's
Hard to tell
Involved custard
Don't ask

Jules:
?
...
I guess you're passed out somewhere...
...
Goodnight, Will

4th April

Jules:
Hi, I heard you're in LA now?

4th April (hours later):

Will:
Sorry. Time difference. Only just woke up.
Yeah, been here a couple of weeks

Jules:
Meet anyone famous?
Jay said you're going to the Oscar parties and things?

Will:
No.
I mean...
I went to one, just to see what it was like
I told the guys that was why I'm here
Easier for them to believe than this Eat Pray Love thing I'm doing
Or less embarrassing anyway

Jules:
Eat Pray Love?
You're on a journey of self-discovery?

Will:

Don't laugh
I don't know
I don't know what I'm doing really
I just needed a change, you know?
To be... by myself for a bit?
Away from the guys
See who I am without them

Jules:
I'm sorry
I'm sorry if it was me who made you feel like that

Will:
No
No, not really...
Maybe a bit. But it's OK.
And anyway...
The guys...
Things were getting messy. Even by their standards
I'd had enough

Jules:
The custard?

Will:
That was the least of it
I wasn't enjoying it?
The life I was living?
That's all I know
Sorry.

I'm not explaining it.
I know I sound weird.

Jules:
No. I get it.
Or I think I do.
Are you OK?

Will:
God, yeah, I'm fine
Totally fine.
Honestly.
I just needed to do something different for a bit.

Jules:
OK. So long as you're OK.

Will:
I am. Absolutely.

Jules:
So you're staying in LA?
Or travelling around?

Will:
Travelling, I guess.
I don't know.
I don't have much of a plan.
Someone invited me over for the parties
Thought I'd start here and see where I ended up

I think I'll head down the coast
Go all the way down to South America
Travel round there for a bit.

Jules:
Wow. That sounds amazing.

Will:
No, it's a spoilt rich kid on a belated gap year

Jules:
OK, I was just being polite

Will:
I know. It freaked me out.
Abuse me, Jules
...
Or not. No pressure.

Jules:
Sorry. I just went to brush my teeth.
It's bedtime here.

Will:
Ah, right.
Of course, yeah.
Goodnight, Jules

Jules:
Goodnight/good morning

Sleep tight
Don't let the Oscar winners bite

27th July

Will:
I'm in Bolivia and I think I just saw Ethan Pennington?

Jules:
Whaaaat?

Will:
Hang on...
Need to check
...
Definitely Ethan
He has me drinking mezcal
This will not end well
...
I think I'm on a plane...
A teeny tiny plane
...

Jules:
Will?
...
?
...

Please don't crash
Will, seriously
...
FFS, please text me back
...
Please
<missed call from Jules Orton>
<missed call from Jules Orton>
<missed call from Jules Orton>

28th July

Will:
Sorry
Had no signal
I'm fine

Jules:
FFS!!
Do not get in tiny rickety planes
Or if you do, don't tell me about it
And DO NOT DIE
It's not allowed
Jay would miss you
He's annoying when he's mopey

Will:
OK. Understood.

I'm being careful. I promise.

14th August

Jules:
How are things?
Haven't heard from you in a while
Just thought I'd check you were alive

Will:
Hello!
Thanks for the check-in
Sorry, I didn't want to keep bothering you

Jules:
You're not bothering me
The opposite
I like hearing from you

Will:
That's nice
Sorry.
Nice is a terrible word
I revoke my claim to being bookish and literary

Jules:
You know I like nice
Anyway. It's too late

Ink and paper are in your blood
I know you for the book nerd you really are
Because I bet you anything you can tell me which literary figure despises the word 'nice'

Will:
Anything?

Jules:
No dirty pictures

Will:
Damn
I'm really in need of some
Piles of laundry, rubbish heaps, muddy boots...

Jules:
That's your fetish, is it?

Will:
I'm too nice to have fetishes ;)

Jules:
Hah.
Yeah, right.

Will:
Henry Tilney, Northanger Abbey

Jules:

Weird fetish, Will

Will:
Damn you, Jules.
You know what I mean.
Tilney is who hates the word nice

Jules:
Correct.
You are a true book nerd, through and through

Will:
Takes one to know one

12th September

Will:
I'm in India

Jules:
God. So predictable.
Don't get a tattoo

Will:
Too late
It says
'I spent three hours in Kinross service station and all I got was this lousy tattoo'

Jules:
OMG! I have the exact same one!
But I'm glad our journey didn't put you off travelling

Will:
It didn't put me off anything
Except the M90

11th October

Will:
I'm in Vienna
In a cafe
You'd like it

Jules:
Is Julie Delphy there?
Are you living out some Before Sunrise fantasy?

Will:
Excellent film, but no…

Jules:
Tell me you're not drinking espresso and writing in a Moleskine notepad
Working on a novel…

Will:
Well...
Actually...

Jules:
OMG
How many naked elf-maidens have appeared so far?

Will:
Sadly none.
And it's not a novel...
Promise not to laugh
Why am I even asking that of you?
OK. So the thing is...
I've been writing a sort of blog about my trip
And I've been too embarrassed to show it to anyone
BUT
Here's the link
...
Suddenly regretting sending this to the most brutal person I know

Jules:
Shut up. It's amazing.
This is seriously your writing?
You write so beautifully, Will

Will:
Really?

Jules:
YES

Will:
OK

Jules:
I mean it.
This is beautiful
Though there's a sad lack of sword fights
And bearded wizards

Will:
I know, I know

Jules:
And romantic entanglements with princesses

Will:
And not a single One Bed trope
No bed sharing of any kind, in fact
Or hammock sharing
Or beach sand under the stars sharing
Or sweaty bus seat sharing
Or suspiciously rusty riverboat sharing

Jules:
Will...

Will:

Unless you count the time I passed out on Ethan's shoulder
And threw up on his shoes

Jules:
So dirty

Will:
Fairly disgusting, yes
But I like to think it precipitated his return to England
So at least I've been of some use to someone

Jules:
Show your writing to people, Will
Please

15th December

Jules:
I heard you're back
Are you going to the Deveron Christmas party?

Will:
I might. Are you going?

Jules:
I think so

Will:
See you there?

Chapter 17

Jules got a lift to Deveron with Jay and Sophia. Which was perfectly fine, and logical, and sensible. And not at all remotely disappointing.

But what would she have even said to Will, had he offered to drive her? She hadn't seen him in a year. She'd heard nothing but sporadic messages, most of them seeming to be sent when he was drunk, or late at night. And what did that mean? Did he only think of her in his idle moments? Or did he only allow himself to message her when his defences were down?

Did he fight it, the urge to speak to her? The way she did? Phone in her hand at night, on the train to work, at her desk, thoughts drifting, following him around the world... Everything she saw and did reminding her of him. *I wonder if Will likes... I'll have to tell Will about... I bet Will would love...*

A year. He'd been gone a year. And would he even be there tonight? Jay said so. Jay said he *thought* so, watching her reaction with amused, knowing eyes.

Dammit.

Because it was hardly the first time she'd asked her

brother about Will. She'd spent a year desperate for news of him, ears pricking whenever his name entered conversation.

"Apparently he's in LA..."

"Did you hear he spotted Ethan Pennington?"

"He's not even coming back for his birthday. Vik's pissed there's going to be no party..."

It wasn't enough.

His infrequent messages weren't enough. The things he said—or more often didn't say. The things she read into them, tried to see between the lines, doubting her own analysis...

None of it was enough. Or only enough to drive her mad.

Just as she'd always suspected, love was basically a mental illness.

Love.

Love.

Love.

She laughed bitterly to herself as she dumped her bag on the bed of her room at Castle Deveron. Her heart had started pounding before they even arrived at the castle. It had been choking her by the time Jay pulled into the courtyard, her eyes scanning the lines of parked cars for a ridiculously over-sized black Bentley Bentayga.

But Ben wasn't there.

He might have a new car. (Irrational how that made her sad.)

He might not have arrived yet.

He might have got a lift with someone else.

He might be here *with* someone else.

What if he had met someone in America, or India, or China, and all those messages he'd sent her had been written with nothing but friendliness, an unseen woman at his side, curled around him in bed?

She might walk down the stairs now, and there he'd be, arm around someone's waist.

But Jay would have said, wouldn't he?

Jay knew. Jay suspected...

Suspected what? That his little sister had a crush?

He might not want to hurt her feelings.

He might not realise how important it was.

He might not realise it was love.

Love.

Hah.

This brutal longing? This desperate hope? Was that love?

No wonder she'd spent her life afraid of it.

She'd moved to London at the start of the year, happy with her job at the tiny publishing house—they specialised in romance; the irony. Happy with her flat: the top floor of a little Victorian terrace, shared with a woman she didn't really know, but who was equally content with that state of affairs. Happy with a whole new life away from Rakely for the first time. Away from her parents, free of their company and their money, and any dependence on them. It was the realisation of a several-year goal.

And a month into it, she'd realised she still wasn't free.

The damage they'd caused her was in her heart. Her soul. Her mind.

The damage stung her every time she recalled that last conversation with Will, sleet burning her frozen skin, tears burning hotter as he drove away. And took her heart with him.

It turned out that love wasn't a risk at all. Because it wasn't even a choice to be made. It happened without permission.

Maybe sometimes it creeps up on you so gradually, you're falling in love before you even realise what's happening—

Maybe sometimes you fall in love over eight years without even realising. Falling for every kind smile from that boy you hardly know, your brother's friend. The quietest one. The shortest one. Maybe you're falling when your house is suddenly full of drunk strangers and music and everyone is jeering and heedless, except that one boy, who smiles, and mouths, "Sorry," and ushers your brother's idiot friends back downstairs. You're falling for blue-grey eyes and faint freckles and the veiled glimpses of a poet's soul. You're falling for the way he loves another. For good-natured teasing and a million types of smile. Maybe you fall because he's patient and he's nice. Maybe you fall because his kiss unlocks your soul. Maybe you fall because it only takes a few hours of conversation for him to become your most favourite person in the world.

Maybe you fall and you're too scared to admit it.

That was the damage she couldn't escape. The scar her upbringing had left inside.

And what it had lost her damaged her further every day.

I wasn't enjoying it. The life I was living. That's all I know.

She went to therapy. She copied Will's Eat Pray Love journey of discovery, but in a small room in South London, with pale yellow walls and a radiator that ticked and a large, dusty fern in one corner.

How she'd hated it. The humiliation of asking for help. Of saying, *Please, please, I can't live like this. I'm broken. I'm lost.*

No cures to be found in the pages of her favourite books. No defence any more in sarcasm and contempt.

No pretending any more.

Just Jules on a chair talking to a woman who seemed scarcely older than her. And who seemed a little bored. And who gave her badly photocopied sheets and a leaking biro and told her to write down her deepest, darkest fears.

But she did the work. Hating it. Needing it. And over weeks, they unpicked it all, took it all out, recognised it, named it. None of it made the things go away, but there is power in names. In knowing the truth of things and bringing them into the light.

Fear. That was one of them.

Trauma.

Doubt.

Insecurity.

Distrust.

Love...

Jules unzipped her garment bag and took out her dress. She hung it on the wardrobe door, scowling at the wrinkles, hoping they'd smooth out in time.

The dress was black, of course. A vintage prom dress. Sleeveless, full-skirted. She'd wear it with her biker boots and too much makeup and hope she was channelling the aura of Courtney Love's dark twin. Because she might be starting to get her head together, but she was still Jules Orton. A fierce, sneering, lipsticked girl who didn't give a shit. Who scoffed at real-life romance and fairytales. Whose heart was closely guarded.

Against everyone except one boy.

The nicest one in the world. The unassuming farm boy type, with the freckles and the heart of gold.

He was the unlikely hero of the story. And he was the only one who had the key.

Chapter 18

Will stood with his hands braced on the balustrade of the Castle Deveron minstrel's gallery and searched the crowd below.

She should be easy to spot. He dreamt of her, thought of her daily. She had the power to make his heart pound and send his thoughts stuttering to a stop.

She also had the power to dig into the deepest parts of his soul and somehow make him laugh his head off while she was doing it.

Divine torment.

Jules Orton.

But he couldn't see her. He'd arrived late, unable to drive up the day before as he'd planned, and the party was already in full swing. He was here now, though, after nearly eight hundred miles of stomach-churning anticipation. After circumnavigating the entire world.

And Jules was not.

Not anywhere he could find, anyway. He was sure she was in the castle somewhere. He'd asked Jay. He'd asked Jay about five times, until his friend began to look at him with amused suspicion playing like smoke in his grey eyes.

Jules *was* here. But where?

And what sort of greeting would he get?

Probably not the one he fantasised about. Jules spotting him across a crowded room, eyes widening, lips parting, flying into his arms... He snorted at the thought. This was *Jules*. She'd probably tell him his traveller's tan made him look like a game show host, or the bow tie of his tux was done wrong. Or his fly was undone.

He quickly checked. It wasn't.

Below him, the party guests milled in the cavernous hall, ancient banners hanging from shadowed rafters beyond the light. The orange glow of the enormous fire spilt like honey over the smooth-trodden flagstones. Red and green: the holly and the ivy. Silver and gold: the dresses and the champagne. Black and white: the tuxes and the dark snow-filled night beyond the thick stone walls.

Music played, voices rolled together as one, and through the crowd, Will saw a familiar face.

Fel.

Fel hadn't seen her. The first words he'd ever really spoken to her. "Is Jules with you?" And she'd just shaken her head and moved on past. He turned around and found his friend.

"Biffy! Sorry, Will," Jay greeted him easily, hand-in-hand with Sophia, who flashed Will a small smile. "I'll get used to it eventually."

"Call me what you want, Jay."

"No. I'll call you what *you* want, Will. Stop pandering to the likes of me. I don't deserve it. Right, Soph?"

"You call *me* Clements."

"Which you *like*," he protested.

She gave her boyfriend a secret smile. But one which Will had no trouble interpreting as: *I like everything you call me.* "It's my surname," she stated.

"I could call you by mine?" offered Jay, making her eyes grow wide and her cheeks turn pink. She looked away, and Jay grinned, quickly kissing the knuckles of her hand before turning back to Will.

Who was standing there feeling very much the third wheel.

"Have you seen—"

"Jules?" finished Jay with the lift of an eyebrow.

Will coloured slightly, but held Jay's knowing look, wondering if they needed to have a talk, man-to-man. Friend to friend. Brother to man-with-hots-for-sister. It seemed premature, though, given he had no idea if Jules would even be happy to see him.

"Hey, Biff!" a man's voice called. "I mean, Will. Catch!"

He turned just in time to awkwardly catch the mass of green leaves someone threw at him. Hugo, standing near the fireplace. He winked. "Early Christmas present. Thought you might need it. Go on," he urged in a faux-whisper. "Go kiss the girl."

"Mm," commented the woman at his side. "Because *that's* never gone wrong."

Hugo laughed, bending to whisper something in her ear, while Will looked at the bundle of leaves. There were white berries nestled among the glossy dark green. Mistletoe, pulled from the winter garland over the fireplace.

He met Jay's eyes.

"Try the library," his friend suggested, and clapped a hand on his shoulder, turning him in that direction and giving him a little push.

Not that he needed it.

But he appreciated it, all the same.

Jules sensed him before she saw him. Which shouldn't really have been possible, but all the chemical brain goo did strange things to a person's faculties.

She was standing in the most gorgeous place she could imagine. A huge old library, towering shelves in a room of ancient wood and even older stone, red and gold rugs on the floor, leather armchairs by a softly crackling fire. The scent of mulled wine rose from her glass on the rosewood table where she was standing studying an exquisite copy of an old, rare book.

But it all faded to nothing when she lifted her eyes to the man who had just walked in.

About average height, about average build. Blue-grey eyes and medium-brown hair, now sun-bleached almost to gold. His skin was tanned, and he looked altogether a little tougher, a little more rugged, a little bit older.

But he looked at her and she saw he was, in essentials, completely unchanged.

Thank God.

"Will."

He smiled in reply. Not false or bland, but like the sunrise, as though it was unstoppable. She took a step around the table towards him, moving on instinct, as though going to him was inevitable too.

But she paused, the gravity of the moment too big, a year's worth of unspoken things hanging in the air like jungle vines between them.

What could she say, when the only thing she wanted to say was everything?

"It's been a while," said Will quite casually with a different sort of smile. Small. Constrained. His manner kept her firmly rooted to the spot, doubting.

Was his heart not stopping his throat? Was he not trembling, thoughts roaring, far too hot in this suddenly airless room?

Was it just her?

"How have you been?" he asked, taking a few more steps into the room, eyes shifting from her to lightly scan the bookshelves. He touched an old globe on one of the side tables, idly turning the world this way and that.

"OK," she said. "You?"

"I've been OK too."

He came over to her table. He looked down at the book she had been leafing through and twisted it towards him with one hand, checking the front cover. "Homer's Odyssey?" He quirked a questioning eyebrow.

"I've become a fan of travel writing."

"Is that so?"

She swallowed. "Yes. Someone convinced me of its value."

His eyes flew to hers, hearing the meaning hidden in her words. "They did?"

Her pulse beat painfully in her throat as she teetered on the precipice of confession. But she looked away.

"How are you? You look good. I mean, you look well. Healthy."

"You look good too, Jules."

She blushed. So much for being the fierce girl. She felt ridiculous, her vintage dress a costume. But when she risked a glance at Will, he was looking at her as though he found her anything but ridiculous.

Blue skies and storms. His eyes both passion and warmth.

She escaped the look, dropping her gaze to the black and white of his tux, the line of his shoulder, the flat plane of his chest, down to his hand...

"What are you holding?"

He flushed. "Mistletoe. Forgot I was carrying it. Hugo's idea of a joke."

"Oh."

He fiddled with it, twining a leaf around a tanned finger.

"Why are you here?" he asked. "And not at the party?"

"Books." She shrugged.

He smiled, nodding, and began leafing through the elaborate, illustrated volume of Homer. But his smile stung, because it was too close to his old one. *I'm fine, everything's fine, don't worry about me...*

"And I'm here because... Because I thought you weren't coming. And I didn't want to be there if you weren't."

"So you did want me to come?"

His question surprised her. "Of course. Why wouldn't I?"

Now his smile turned crooked, fell short. He aimed it anywhere but her. "We didn't... We didn't part on good terms."

"Will... I've spent a whole year missing you."

"As a friend? Or..."

He cut himself off, annoyed, she thought, at the clumsy way he was pressing her. But her heart leapt, gave her hope.

"I did mean to come up yesterday," he said quickly, burying his last words under the explanation. "But I was stuck in London for a meeting. Then there wasn't quite enough time."

"You drove up today?"

"Yes. Arrived an hour ago."

"You must be tired."

"No, I'm..." He broke off, toyed with the book again, seeming as frustrated as her that they were stuck on this commonplace, meaningless exchange. "I'm not tired."

From somewhere nearby came the raucous sound of a piano, a few bars of a country jig, a stroke of the keyboard, a blues scale or two. The sound of people having fun, reminding them they were at a party.

"Will... You left. For a year."

She hated the way her voice wobbled. How much it revealed about what she had suffered. But honesty was good, her therapist said. Openness and trust and letting yourself be vulnerable...

Will nodded, the movement heavy, as though he felt the

justice of what she said. Her words a sentence he deserved.

"I said something to you about taking risks the last time we spoke. That was mine. A year to get to know myself. To know my own mind. To prove..."

He stopped on an exhale as though his courage had failed him. Rubbing a hand across his jaw, he set his shoulders and tried again. "To prove I did know my own mind. What I wanted. What I felt." He looked at her fleetingly, lashes lowered. His hand reached for the book on the table and it was trembling, the movement clumsy. "You didn't believe me, and you were right not to, I don't blame you, but please tell me there was a point to it, because being away from you was the hardest thing I've ever done—"

Her breath caught.

"I didn't do it to hurt you," he continued, words stumbling now, as though he was running out of time, out of air. "I did it for you. For us. For there to be a chance *of* us. You once asked me if I'd really travel eight hundred miles just to see Fel's face... Jules, I've travelled around the entire world just for the chance that you might give me a chance... This isn't me asking you for something in return. I'm not trying to guilt you into anything or prove anything to you except the truth of it. I've spent every day of the last year feeling exactly as I did on the day we parted. That I want to take this risk with you. The risk of finding out if this can be the ever-lasting certain-beyond-any-doubt thing that you're waiting for... But if you don't feel the same—"

"Will—" It was a sob more than his name.

"If you don't feel the same, Jules, it's OK. All I wanted was to give you a chance to say yes. To feel like I'm a risk that might be worth taking." He ran a hand down his face again. "God, sorry. I didn't mean to say all that. I meant to play it cool, give you time... I'm an idiot. My hands are shaking..."

She came all the way around the table to where he was standing and took hold of his hands. "Mine are shaking too."

He gasped a laugh at that, looking down, too wrought to meet her eyes. Her whole body was shaking. Her palms were damp, her stomach twisting. Every word in the world had flown her mind. *What did you say when you needed to say everything...*

She tried to twine her fingers into his. The mistletoe was still clutched in his left hand. With a clumsy, nervous grip, she tore a sprig free and tucked it into the buttonhole of his jacket.

"I'm so glad you're here."

He met her eyes. "You are?"

"Of course I am. Apparently there's a train strike tomorrow."

He huffed a broken laugh. "Need a lift, do you?"

"Will..." She set her hand on his chest by the mistletoe, feeling the thick fabric of his jacket, the muscle below, the pounding heart below that. "What I need...is you."

For a moment, he was frozen, motionless, eyes searching hers as though he didn't quite believe, wasn't quite sure—

She leant up and kissed him.

Just on the cheek.

But her mouth lingered against his skin, unable to leave. She found the nape of his neck, drew his mouth to hers.

He exhaled shakily as her lips brushed his, and his breath sounded like her name.

"Jules..."

He kissed her back, chest rising as he moved to meet her mouth. His hands curled into her hair, tilting her head so he could deepen the kiss, taste her fully, meeting her desperate need with his own.

He moved one hand down her body, pulling her firmly against him. She moaned at the contact, her fears swallowed by maddening desire as their kiss turned breathless and wild. She pushed her hands under his jacket, its silk lining warmed by his body, the fine fabric of his waistcoat tightly encasing firmly muscled ribs.

But he drew back as she reached for his button, holding her head in his palms, forehead against hers.

"Tell me this means something," he gasped. "That it's not just..."

She felt the fear, both their fears. That it might mean too much. That it might not mean enough. It pierced her chest, the sharp twist of a knife. But the gap it made pooled warm and alive, spreading through her, choking her voice.

"Will... It means everything."

Chapter 19

Her silver eyes held his steady as the accumulated hopes of a twelvemonth suddenly found their footing. It was painful, the way they clawed at him, those ancient dragons—love and hope—as old as time, settling in his ribs, claws grasping heedlessly as they held on to those words.

It means everything.

He looked at Jules, heart beating in time with dragon wings, wondering if he dared believe what he hoped. Because if he was wrong, that same hope would tear him apart. But...

It's always going to be a risk. Falling in love.

That's what he'd told her, angry and hurt. But he understood now what it was like, to fear you could lose everything.

It didn't stop him leaping from the rock face.

"I love you."

She stared back at him. He said it again.

"I love you."

Idiot farm boy. Too stupid to live, sacrificing himself because he realised he needed to say it first, hold her hand, smooth her path, take the lead. And now she just stared at him, and he was falling, falling, falling...

Until she said, "I love you too."

"Really?"

She nodded, touching his face, the line of his jaw. Her eyes followed the path of her fingers, and he remembered the time she had bathed the graze on his cheek when he fell. Was she remembering it too?

"You said I needed to take a risk..." Her voice was quiet, speaking secret thoughts. "I was scared of what I felt, trying to protect myself. But it turned out it wasn't even a choice for me to make. I had no control over it. Love comes, and it takes—"

"And it gives." He took hold of her hands. "It gives. I know you're scared, Jules. But we're doing this together."

"But no one knows what's going to happen—"

"Well, true. I suppose I could get hit by a bus..."

She shoved him with the push of her thigh.

"Or crash a rickety plane in the Bolivian jungle—"

"Don't. Don't joke about that."

"But I'm planning on loving you forever. I want to get disgustingly old, and hairy in all the wrong places, and bald in all the others, and bore you to death decade after decade..."

"This is getting decidedly less romantic by the minute."

He chuckled. "OK. Let me borrow another person's words. Something I read once."

Still holding her hands, he got down on his knees. Her eyes widened, mouth opening in a silent protest—then clamping back a tear-filled laugh as she recognised the words he was reciting.

"*I could say that I would rehang the stars for you, but you wouldn't care for such nonsense, fierce-heart. Instead, I promise to walk every road in the world with you. I go where you go. You are my Queen now, the only country I need. This is how it must be. Our two hearts are pinned. They beat as one.*"

"Oh my God. You memorised the prince's speech."

"It *was* the only book I took with me when I left the country. I read it fifteen times."

"It's not even the best one."

"*Now* you tell me."

"Get up, you idiot."

She tugged on his hands, and he came back to his feet, his smile shaky as he looked down at her. "In my own, inadequate words: You're the smartest, funniest woman I've ever met. I'm slightly frightened of you. You drive me insane. You make the world light up. You are brain-meltingly gorgeous. And you see me, somehow. Somehow, you *see* me. Jules… I've spent every day of the last year missing you like crazy, and every day of it loving you. And the only thing that's going to change is that I might learn to love you even more." He grinned. "Especially in this dress. With these boots."

Tears filled her eyes, and she dropped her head to his chest, his arms coming around her. Just one of those ordinary, everyday miracles: a man holding the woman he loved.

She muffled a half-laughing groan against his chest. "This isn't fair. I can't make romantic speeches. The space-time continuum would break if I got on my knees and said flowery things. I'll just have to show you instead."

"Show me...on your knees?" he enquired hopefully.

She smacked his chest with another groan. "Will! That was me trying to be romantic."

"I know. It was disconcerting. But..." He squeezed her more tightly. "I absolutely loved it."

They walked from the library, shyly hand-in-hand.

They found the source of the music in the wide vestibule at the foot of a staircase. A gleaming black grand piano was half-tucked into the space under the curving flight of stone steps, a small crowd gathered round it.

Jules recognised the blond-haired man at the keys. Tom Brewerly, who had, for a time, been Castle Deveron's steward. He flipped the hair back from his eyes with a toss of his head as he played, his rich baritone bubbling with laughter. He was singing in French, his performance aimed at the pink-haired woman leaning by the piano, regarding him with a look half-entranced, half-bemused, as though wondering how on earth this was her life.

"*Non Regrette Rien?*" commented Jules in an undertone. "That's not even a Christmas song."

"I suspect the only other one he knows is *Frère Jacques*," Will whispered, making her laugh.

They had paused near the foot of the stairs. Other couples were there, leaning against each other. She felt the half-foot of space between her and Will, acutely conscious of their joined hands, their one point of contact.

She wanted to lean into him. She wanted his arms around her, holding her as he had done in the library. But it was all so new, electric and fizzing, sparky and jittering. An arrhythmic heart pounding.

She needed him, wanted him, even more than she had that night in the hotel, lying so close in the dark with the threads of her sanity unspooling as she tried to come up with any good reason not to give in.

His thumb brushed her wrist. Her eyes flashed to his.

"I got you a present," he murmured, only just audible over the music.

"Really?"

"Of course I did. It's Christmas. It's in my room though."

"God. Is this some line?" she blustered, heart racing. "You're going to get me there and really it's your penis?"

He burst out laughing, then quickly stopped, shooting an apologetic look toward the piano. But he leant down and whispered against her ear. "That's my back-up present."

"I hope it's wrapped."

"With an *enormous* bow."

She swallowed, keeping her eyes on the piano performance. "Well. I do like presents."

"Even with your Scrooge-like nature?"

"I'm fine with the commercial exchange aspects of Christmas."

"It's just the sentimentality you don't like?"

"Exactly."

"Most people are the other way around."
"I'm not most people."
"No. True."
"Will?"
"Yes?"
"Shut up and give me my present."
"Yes, Jules."
He led the way upstairs.

Will's room was in one of the towers, and as they climbed round and round the curving stone steps up into the quiet, private parts of the house, Jules suspected she looked much like Tom Brewerly's pink-haired girlfriend. Dazed and bemused, no real idea how life had brought her to this moment.

Sudden, dizzying happiness was hard to get one's head around. Will's words in the library kept echoing in her mind. Will's face, his voice, her own...

I love you.

I love you too.

There was no going back now. There never had been. When he left last Christmas, he drove away with her heart in his pocket. Dragged it all around the world. Nearly broke it with his silence and his absence. And that terrifying night he got into a plane and didn't reply...

She'd known then, as though she hadn't already, that she loved him. Was chock-full of that brain goo. That irrational, terrifying illness. This must be the manic stage. The delirium. Because she didn't have a single straight thought in her head. They were wheeling and rushing and swimming and spinning, and as they grew closer to Will's room, she found it harder and harder to breathe, to think at all, to be conscious of anything but the man at her side, his body, his hand in hers and the beating of his pulse against her fingertips.

"Machu Picchu was easier to climb," said Will as they mounted another turn in the stairs.

She laughed, her voice ringing off the stone. *Hah-hah-hah.* Definitely mad. Hysterical, even.

They got to his door, walked into his room. A semi-circular space, old tapestries on stone walls, and a dark, four-poster bed, a brocade coverlet folded at the base over crisp, white sheets.

Will let go of her hand and crossed over to the bed where his bag was half-unzipped. He rummaged through it for a moment, then came back holding a present wrapped in dark blue paper with silver snowflakes, tied with a silver bow.

"You really did get me a present," she said as he handed it to her.

"Of course."

She turned it over in her hands. It was neatly wrapped, but not quite perfectly enough to have been wrapped in store. Had he done it himself? Her heart felt wobbly and strange at the thought.

Stupid brain goo.

"A book," she said, already sure before she got the first

corner unwrapped. Then she stopped and glanced up guiltily. "Can I open it now?"

He was biting his lip, laughing at her a little. "Yes, Jules."

When she tore the rest of the paper off, she stared. "But this... This isn't out yet!" She looked a little closer, turning the chunky paperback over in her hands. "This is a review copy, the advanced one. It's not out for months."

"After reading the first one fifteen times, I was pretty eager to find out what happened next."

"Have you read it?"

"No. It's for you."

"But... But how...?"

He smiled, clearly pleased to have pleased her. "It helps to know a lot of people who know a lot of people."

"Ugh. People."

He laughed. "They're not all bad."

"No." She looked at him, smiling. "They're not."

"But I guess now you can spend the rest of the party in your room reading..."

"I thought you had another present for me?"

He met her look, cheeks heating as she put the book to one side and took a step towards him. "Or was that just an empty promise? You bring a girl all the way up here, to this room with only one bed..."

He glanced back at it, did an exaggerated double-take. "How did that get there? I could have *sworn* I ordered a twin..."

"Will?"

"Yes?"

"Is it still romantic if I just take all my clothes off and

climb you like a tree?"

"Erm. I think... Yes. I'd be OK with that."

"Well, you are the romance expert..."

Heart racing, channelling all the confidence the heat in his eyes gave her, she reached behind and slid down the zip of her dress. The feral hunger with which he watched her push the dress from her body made her stomach flip. She remembered it from their night together. Had sometimes thought maybe it was a dream, the way it tortured her in the night... But, no. She hadn't imagined it. She'd only forgotten quite how intense it was.

Her dress fell to the floor, the black silk sliding down her body.

"Black," muttered Will, almost a curse. But it wasn't her dress that had forced the word from him. His gaze dragged from her black bra to her black knickers as she stepped towards him.

The thick fabric of his tux met her bare skin, buttons scraping across her stomach as she pressed herself closer, rising on her toes to touch her lips to the slight scratching stubble of his jaw.

"Fuck, Jules. You fucking kill me."

She linked her hands behind his neck. "You're not touching me, Will."

He squeezed his eyes shut as though in pain. "I'll die."

She breathed a laugh, grazed her mouth down the taut line of his throat. "Is it still romantic if I ask you to fuck me the way you're looking at me? As though I'm some dream girl and you're losing your mind?"

He groaned, but his hand came gently to her face,

knuckle brushing her cheek. "I could never have dreamed anyone like you."

She nipped his thumb with her lips. "Not sure that's a compliment, Will."

He laughed softly, and his hand flattened against her cheek, bringing her to his mouth. "Of course it's a compliment," he said against her lips, before kissing her, full and soft and taking, moving deeper with each slide of his mouth, until she was melting against him, weak and dizzy, his kiss making her fall apart just as surely as it had done the last time.

He stroked his hands down her back and pulled her to him. His hardness ground against her front, and she whimpered, helpless with need.

"How wet are you, Jules?" He kissed her throat, pulling the straps of her bra from her shoulders as her head tipped back. "Do you remember? In the hotel?" He scattered kisses over her shoulders, the base of her throat. "You said you were wet just thinking about me. Do you know how many times I've replayed that in my mind?"

She tried to speak, but he had teased her nipples free from her bra, and his thumb was swiping back and forth as he kissed the corner of her throat. He snapped the clasp of her bra and tossed it aside.

"How wet, Jules? Tell me."

"Wet..."

"Soaking?"

"Yes..."

He made a noise of approval, then walked her to the bed. He was in charge now. And she realised how much she liked this, letting him kiss the fierce girl into submission, tame the dragon, take control. She trusted him to know what she would like. They were two hearts beating as one... She was his and he was hers, and he could do anything, anything...

She stood, lust-drunk, at the edge of the bed as Will pulled her knickers down, lifted them from her feet. He stood and kissed her again, kissing her down, melting her like wax to pool underneath him on the bed.

He was braced over her, kneeling with one thigh between hers. "Show me how wet you are," he whispered. "Please."

She spread her legs as he sat back, his eyes moving down. He let out a low noise, a sound of appreciation so filthy it made her insides clench, a jolt of desire that ricocheted from her clit to her belly and back again.

"Fuck, Jules." He dragged a finger through the slickness at her core. "Did I do this to you?"

She could only gasp. His touch felt too good. She was already too close to the edge. And Will was still fully dressed, ridiculously handsome in his dark evening wear, his tan golden against the white of his shirt.

She pulled him down to her by the lapel of his suit, pushing his jacket from his shoulders, dragging at the buttons of his waistcoat. He helped her, shucking his waistcoat, unbuttoning his shirt, but pressing his thigh between her legs as he looked down at her, satisfaction in his eyes as she started to move against him, taking whatever friction she could get.

Will unbuckled his belt, started on his fly, watching her

grind helplessly against his knee.

"Could you come like that?"

"Yes, but..."

He leant forwards, angling his knee deeper against her as he bent down to kiss her mouth, her breasts. "But what?" His tongue swirled around her nipple, then he sucked, and it nearly sent her over the edge.

"But I want you inside me. Please, Will. I want you."

"OK..." He kissed her neck, voice hoarse. "OK."

He climbed off the bed, and she watched, drugged, as he took the rest of his clothes off and found a condom in his wallet. She pulled him back to her greedily. He paused, thighs between hers, chest brushing her nipples as he kissed her.

She reached down, took the heat and width of him in her hand. He moaned, burying his face against her neck as she stroked him, his hips moving irresistibly, thrusting into her grip.

"It's been a year, Jules," he groaned. "I'm not going to last if you keep that up."

"Has it?" she whispered. "Has it really been a year?"

He lifted his head to look into her eyes, knowing what she was asking. What the frightened, fragile part of her needed to know.

"There's been no one else, Jules. I'm yours. Utterly yours."

He kissed her deeply and she pulled him to her, legs wrapped around his as she urged him inside. They moved together, and her arms wrapped around him too, around his shoulders and the muscle of his back. He rocked into her, the slide, the stretch, the friction just right. She wrapped all of him in the love she felt. And she finally, fully, unwrapped her heart.

Epilogue

Christmas Day, Herlingcote

Jules woke on Christmas morning, naked and tangled in Will's arms. He was also spooning her from behind *and* had one hand splayed possessively across her bare stomach. She'd suspect him of having taken notes from the book he'd given her for Christmas, but, in truth, he was just a natural.

This was the third such morning. The first had been at Deveron, the day after the party. The second, on Christmas Eve, after a night spent at their favourite hotel, breaking the journey to here, Herlingcote, William's family home in Berkshire.

"Where are you spending Christmas?" he'd asked her, as they lay lazily together in the bed at Castle Deveron.

"Not Fel's," she'd said, needing to voice the name out loud, at least once, just to get it over with. "Not this year. Her mother has been sick, and everyone's been so busy... Besides, I haven't seen much of her recently. I think we've...grown apart a bit."

Her head had been nestled on his shoulder, his fingers stroking the line of her arm. He'd stilled momentarily, then drawn her tighter against him. "I'm sorry."

"No, no, nothing like that. We've not fallen out or anything. Just... Maybe it's because I'm working and living in London now, and she's still up at Edinburgh finishing her course... I haven't managed to visit her much. And... Well... Have you ever had the feeling you're putting more into a friendship than you're getting out?"

His slight laugh had been dry. "Story of my life."

He'd asked where she was going to go instead and when she'd shrugged and said Rakely, he'd said no. "No, not there. Jules..."

He hadn't needed to say anything more.

"My parents won't be there. They're stealing some sun abroad."

"But Jay's going to Leicestershire with Sophia to visit her dad."

"Yes, and Jess will be at Matt's. So, it'll be perfect. I'll have the place to myself."

"With no company but your terrifying housekeeper?"

"She's not there. My parents always send the staff off if they're not there."

"You'd literally be alone on Christmas?"

"See? Perfect for me."

But she was lying, of course. The thought of it made her want to cry like a child.

"Spend it with me, Jules. Or I'll spend it with you. You're not going to be alone."

So, here they were, at the sweeping grandeur of Herlingcote, in its picture-perfect grounds, being welcomed yesterday evening by Will's parents with such obvious delight—and politely veiled curiosity—that she'd gone almost mute, terrified to say the wrong thing and reveal that the woman William had shepherded into his family Christmas was nothing but a disappointing *Orton*—one of those wrong'uns.

She shifted position slightly, tugging the duvet further down, because William was radiating heat, his naked body firmly pressed down the length of hers. The light in the room was pewter-dark, all its objects shades and shadows. She'd seen it yesterday in the afternoon's fading light, a glorious amber sunset framed by the four tall windows that spanned the room's length. It must be two rooms knocked into one; such a broad, airy space. A private palace for the Shilstones' only child. No wonder the boy who grew up here would feel open to the whole world, would dream of space and travel. From his bed, set on the wall facing the windows, you could see the whole sky. She imagined the summer, imagined waking to lacy-white sunlight and a sea of blue over the endless green of the rolling park.

For now, she was happy to curl safe and warm in the middle of the snowy white linen, William at her back. His breathing was soft and even, the forearm wrapped around her waist a solid, comforting weight.

She stroked her palm down the neat muscle of it, the light too dim to see the details, but she was able to picture the cinnamon dusting of freckles, the golden-brown hair that bent under her palm. She ran her hand down to the corded strength of his wrist, and took his hand, raised it to her lips, his arm brushing over her breast. He stirred slightly, breathing deeper, and she shifted back until the promising hardness fell snugly into place between her cheeks.

Lazy, delicious heat unfurled in her stomach, the memory and the anticipation of pleasure. She would have been happy to lie like that for hours, but her movement must have woken him.

"Merry Christmas," he said, voice husky with sleep. He pressed a kiss to the back of her neck, and bright tingles shot down her spine, joining the heat curling low in her belly.

"Merry Christmas."

She turned in his arms, sorry to lose the contact but needing to look at him. He smiled sleepily, eyes dipping unapologetically to her breasts.

"Already the best Christmas ever."

She rolled her eyes. "So easily pleased."

"I'm a simple man."

"Physically maybe, but mentally..."

He chuckled, reaching for her, but she wriggled away and out of the bed. "I've got something for you."

"That's funny. I've got something for you. It's in this bed..."

"Yes, yes, we'll get to your back-up present later."

Will switched on the bedside light as she crossed to her bag. He was watching her every naked move. She enjoyed it hugely. "Here." She knelt back on the bed. "A real present. Wrapped and everything."

He sat up, smiling like a boy, even as he lifted an eyebrow

in confusion. "But when did you get a chance to buy this?"

"I brought it with me to Deveron."

"But you acted so surprised that I'd got you a present!"

"Well... Yes... But I didn't even know if you liked me or hated me. Whereas I was desperately in love with you."

He smiled. "Desperately?"

"Insanely. Nothing but goo. Stop fishing for compliments and open it. Although it's not as good as yours."

"Mine *was* pretty amazing."

She smacked him on his bare shoulder as he laughed, peeling back the paper. He took out a Moleskine notepad and an extremely nice—even if she did say so herself—silver pen. He twisted the pen silently for a moment, studied the nib move, his expression unreadable.

Her heart beat uncomfortably. "What? You hate it? Say something."

"No... God... I love it." When he met her eyes, she saw the emotion swimming in his.

"You need to write, Will. Write whatever you want. Whether it's stuff about swords and hot elf girls, or travelling the world, or seducing weirdos with literary analysis—"

"All of my favourite things."

"You need to write. You're so good at it."

"Come here." He put the pen and pad down and hugged her to him. "Thank you. So much."

"It's nothing," she said awkwardly, embarrassed now.

"I need to tell you something." He sat back, taking one of her hands in his and looking up shyly from lowered lashes.

"You drunkenly got married in Vegas?"

"No. Well, only that one time... Joking. That was Vik. No... The reason I was stuck in London the other day was because I had a meeting with someone from a travel magazine. They're thinking of publishing some of the articles I wrote on my blog, turning them into a series. I need to rework them, of course—"

"Oh my God! That's amazing."

"And they're not really paying me anything—"

"You don't need the money, Will!"

"No, but... I think writers deserve to get paid, don't they? It sets a bad precedent working for free. Not everyone's as fortunate as I am."

"God. Stop being so nice. And thoughtful. And fair-minded."

"I'm trying." He grinned, gently pinching her knee. "Learning from the master."

"It's hopeless, Will. You'll never be anything but a nice guy."

"Can you live with that?"

She shrugged. "I suppose so. If I have to."

He laughed softly, and then he seemed to remember that they were naked. Or that she was. He looked at her, a sweep of his eyes, hunger igniting.

"Lie down, Jules."

She did as she was told.

He moved over her, arms braced, looking down at her face, all sweetness and heat. Naughty and nice.

"Don't you dare kiss me," she warned, as the air between them charged with an already familiar intensity of desire.

"We haven't brushed our teeth."

He grinned, albeit a little wickedly. "Wouldn't think of it, Jules. Or at least..." He kissed her forehead, the tenderness of the action at odds with the gleam in his eyes. "Not on your mouth."

She huffed out a breath of pretend annoyance, pretending, too, not to shiver and tremble as his lips skated her jaw, her throat, her collarbone...

"This is the best story," he said as his mouth skimmed over her skin. "The story of us. Let's write it forever."

His kisses continued to trail down, down, as she wrapped her fingers into the silk of his hair.

"As long as you give me a happy ending."

His laughter tickled her thigh. "Loads of happy endings. Every single day."

Outside, unseen by either, the snow began to fall, kissing the world just as softly, and just as sweet.

Thank you

Thank you so much for reading! If you'd like to sign up for my newsletter and get some freebies, including access to the subscriber-only area of my website, please visit www.rachelrowan.com.

If you liked the book, could you help spread the love? Leaving a review on Amazon is incredibly helpful to us indie authors. We have no marketing budget (and, in my case, no marketing skills!) so we really do depend on word of mouth. Posting about it on social media or recommending it to your friends is also incredibly helpful.

Do stay in touch to find out about new releases—follow me on Amazon, or Instagram, or join my newsletter. Or email me just to say hi! I'd love to hear from you!

Email: rachel@rachelrowan.com

Instagram: @rachelrowanwriter

Website: www.rachelrowan.com

Thank you again for reading! I hope to see you here again at the end of the next book!

Have you tried...?

There are lots more stories in the *Entitled Love* world:

Engaging the Enemy

Hugo Blackton is fairly sure Amelia Banberry-Thompson is never going to forgive him for what he did at her sister's engagement party. Which is unfortunate for several reasons.

One: His father has just banished him from his jet-set playboy lifestyle to manage the family country estate—an estate which borders Amelia's own.

Two: Amelia is one of his oldest friends and life's just not the same if he can't go next door to annoy her. But she's refusing to even see him.

Three: Hugo has just discovered an ancestor once sought to unite the families. Now there's an unclaimed marriage settlement worth millions, and it's his for the taking...if only he can get Amelia to stop hating him long enough to say "I do."

Amelia may have spent her life secretly loving Hugo Blackton, but she knows better than anyone how spoilt and selfish he is. And she definitely knows better than to ever trust him again.

Luckily, Amelia has the perfect distraction from regrets and heartbreak: a stately home on the brink of ruin. Unluckily, the only person willing to help is the last person she wants to see. But for once in his life, Hugo seems oddly determined to say sorry...

The Entitled Love Collection

Four irresistible stories full of heat, humour, and heart, now available together in paperback and ebook for the first time—with new, exclusive bonus epilogues. Discover the banter, romance, and sizzling steam of Entitled Love: modern romcoms with regency-style heroes.

Uncommon
When the arrogant playboy Earl of Lansbury pays an actress to be his fake date he doesn't bargain on learning an uncomfortable life lesson: money can't buy everything. And it definitely can't buy her...

Unspoken
The brooding Duke of Cumbria has spent years fighting what he feels for his best friend's sister. But when circumstances bring her to his lakeside estate for one long, hot summer, the duke finds it increasingly difficult to keep his distance...

Untouched
Shy and socially awkward Sophia needs lessons in love—of the horizontal kind. Who better to ask than her rakish neighbour, the viscount's son? But despite having all the experience, Jay still has a lot to learn about the heart...

Unwanted
Disinherited and penniless, viscount Tom Brewerly has no option but to leave his life in France for a crumbling Scottish castle. The arrival of beautiful artist Laura feels like a miracle—until he discovers she's the best friend of the woman who destroyed his life...

All available on Amazon and Kindle Unlimited. Plus, get a free short story when you sign up for the Rachel Rowan newsletter: www.rachelrowan.com

Books mentioned in Unwrapped

Like Jules and Will, I am a total book nerd. So here is a list of all the books mentioned in Unwrapped. Because I like lists. And books. (I'm a *nerd* nerd.)

Northanger Abbey - Jane Austen
Pride and Prejudice - Jane Austen
Tenant of Wildfell Hall - Anne Brontë
Jane Eyre - Charlotte Brontë
Wuthering Heights - Emily Brontë
Eat, Pray, Love - Elizabeth Gilbert
The Odyssey - Homer
On the Road - Jack Kerouac
The Life and Opinions of Tristram Shandy, Gentleman - Laurence Sterne (Vikram's nickname for his friend Tristan is 'Tristan Shady' - a play on the name Tristam Shandy)
The Picture of Dorian Gray - Oscar Wilde

The fantasy authors Will mentions reading:
- J.R.R. Tolkein (The Lord of the Rings)

- Robert Jordan (The Wheel of Time)

- Brandon Sanderson (Mistborn etc)

The *"it's a fantasy, not a romance"* book that Jules is secretly a fan of is, of course, inspired by several famous romantasy books. I suspect most of you will be able to guess which ones. It's also loosely based on my own fantasy series - one which I vaguely planned out a long time ago, but which, like Will, I suspect I shall never finish writing.

Acknowledgements

As always, thank you so much to my husband and children. You are the joys of my life! Thank you especially to my husband for your patience – I wrote this one to a really tight timeline and there was a lot of panic going on!

Huge thanks to my beta readers Charis, Brianna, and Starla. You're more than beta readers, of course. You are true friends to me and my writing, and I would probably have given up by now if it wasn't for your support!

Last, but definitely not least, thank you so much to YOU, the reader. I'm always so humbled, amazed, and grateful that anyone reads the words I write. Thank you for giving my characters a new home inside your head! I hope their story brought you fun and joy.

Printed in Great Britain
by Amazon